One in Three Hundred

BY J. T. McINTOSH

ONE IN THREE HUNDRED

BORN LEADER

WORLD OUT OF MIND

SATURDAY, NOVEMBER 2, 1991

BY J. T. McINTOSH

One in Three Hundred

Doubleday & Company, Inc.

Garden City, New York, 1954

Library of Congress Catalog Card Number 54–9186

Contents

One in Three Hundred

1

I ignored the half-human thing that ran at my heels like a dog crying, "Please! Please! Please!" I ignored it, except when I had to strike its arm from mine, because that was the only thing to do.

I was twenty-eight, Lieutenant Bill Easson, and a more unremarkable young man it would have been difficult to find. But now, through no fault of my own, I was a god.

I'm not going to try to tell the whole story of those last three weeks. That would fill a library. So if you're looking for some big thing you know about and find it isn't even mentioned, or wonder how I'm going to explain this or that, and find I don't, remember I had a job to do and had no time to stand and stare.

When I reached the main street of Simsville (pop. 3261) I was soon rid of the poor wretch at my heels. Two loungers swept him away when they recognized me. I don't know what they did with him. I didn't ask. I never saw him again.

Pat Darrell joined me, automatically. She didn't even say, "Hullo."

A little over two weeks before, when I came to Simsville, she had been the first person to speak to me. "It's all right," she had assured me at once, "I'm just naturally friendly. I don't want what everyone else wants. At least, I don't expect to get it. So you can write that off, for a start."

Naturally I had been suspicious, believing this to be a new play for the same old stake. Everybody wants to live. And what I brought with me, no more and no less, was the power of life and death.

But I had found that Pat meant exactly what she said. She was the most sincere person I ever met. She had come to accept long since the fact that she just wasn't lucky. She never won anything. When she told me this I asked curiously, "Even beauty competitions?"

"Second," she murmured briefly, as if that explained everything. In a way it did.

As we walked, Fred Mortenson favored us with a jaunty wave from the other side of the street. Mortenson was Pat's opposite. He knew he was going to live; it wasn't worth even considering anything else. He had been lucky so often with so many things that there just couldn't be anything wrong this time, the most important of all.

Mortenson was right; so was Pat.

Our choice must be representative, they had told us. No one wanted a new world with everyone exactly the same age, so that in a few years' time there would only be people of forty and young children, and later only old people and youngsters just reaching nubility. So we had been instructed

10

to pick out a representative selection of ten people who seemed to deserve to live.

Our instructions were as casual as that. Some people were never able to grasp the idea. They frowned and talked about psych records and medical histories, and started back in righteous horror when one of us told them what they could do with their records and histories. These people were back-seat drivers. They weren't doing the thing, but of course they knew how it should have been done.

I had decided on my list early, prepared to revise it as various things happened, as they no doubt would. It seemed the best way to work—I could watch the people I had chosen and confirm their selection or change my mind. The list had changed rapidly in the first few days, but not much since then.

Mortenson was on it. Pat wasn't.

The Powells were on it too, though no one knew that but me. Naturally I kept my plans to myself. We saw the Powells just before we entered Henessy's, and stopped to pass the time of day.

Marjory Powell told me it was a nice day. I agreed gratefully. The Powells, Pat, and Sammy Hoggan were the only people in the village who could treat me as an ordinary human being. Jack Powell was one of those tall, quiet characters with an easy grin. Marjory, without being ugly, was so unbeautiful that she had been able to resign all claims of that kind long ago and concentrate on being a person.

Pat liked them, and so did I. We stood and talked contentedly, and only the knowledge that anyone I spent a lot of time with was marked out for active hatred and jealousy made me take Pat's arm after a few minutes and propel her into the bar.

The Powells didn't seem much affected by the shadow that hung over the world. Their outlook was that the thing was going to come anyway, and they might as well carry on with their usual occupations and hope for the best.

The atmosphere in Henessy's changed perceptibly when we went in. That happened everywhere.

Old Harry Phillips was there, and Sammy Hoggan, in-evitably. They waved cheerfully to Pat and me. The others merely glowered, like children told to be on their best be-havior and immediately thrown on their worst.

We joined Sammy. Though he had taken the disaster badly, there were a lot of worse ways he might have taken it. He never talked about it. He was going to be drunk for the rest of his life. He was the kind of drinker who merely sat without change of expression and pickled his kidneys.

"Hallo, friends," he said. "*O tempora! O mores! Ave atque vale.*"

"I understood the first two words," Pat admitted cau-tiously.

"That's all my Latin, honey, so you'll understand anything else I may say."

I was going to buy him a drink, but he begged me not to. "I'm just hoping Henessy doesn't get some sense and realize money doesn't matter any more," he told us. "Because if he doesn't, I'll soon come to the end of this jag. I haven't much money left."

This wasn't surprising, the way he had been drinking ever since I arrived in town. But Pat frowned.

"You want to come to the end of the jag?" she repeated. "Then why don't you stop?"

"To the simple," Sammy sighed, "all things are simple." He killed his drink without noticing it. "No offense, honey. But it's like this. If I'd only had a few dollars on me four weeks ago, I'd only have been able to take a short dive into the rot-gut. But I was out of luck. I had enough to keep me going for four weeks."

"Four weeks?" I demanded. "Then . . . ?"

It was seven weeks since it passed beyond doubt that the end of the world, which had been prophesied so often, was really fixed this time. Two weeks and two days since I started the job of picking out the ten people in Simsville who were to live.

With the occasionally uncanny directness of the very

drunk, Sammy read my thoughts. "You think I'm drinking because the world's coming to an end?" he asked. He burst out laughing. "God, no. Let it end any time it wants to. Four days now, isn't it? Suits me."

He could talk clearly and soberly when he was sitting down, and raise his glass steadily. But as he got up he was at once obviously very drunk. He staggered away to take some of the weight off his kidneys.

Henessy brought our drinks indifferently. He had no hopes of being one of the ten. He looked on his profession with gloomy disdain. Who would take a bartender to Mars? So, like the Powells, he went on in his own way: business as usual. But I liked the Powells. For some reason I couldn't like Henessy.

Harry joined us. Harry was notable for his craggy features, his fatalistic philosophy, his imperturbability, and his beautiful granddaughter. Bessie Phillips, at eight, was such a lovely child and had such a sunny nature that I hadn't been able to keep her off my list. I couldn't condemn Bessie to death.

If I'd been asked to justify every selection (but I wouldn't be), Bessie was the only one I'd have to rationalize about. I could produce reasons, just as anyone else rationalizing can produce reasons, but the real one was simply that I wanted to take Bessie and I could. Some other lieutenant would include an old lady because she looked like his mother. Someone else would have good reasons to explain why he was taking along one particular fourteen-year-old boy and not one of thirty or forty others; the last he'd produce, if he had to produce any, would be that the boy reminded him of the kid brother who died under the wheels of a truck.

Wrong? Sure, if you're still laboring under the idea that the way to do this was selection on the basis of psych records and medical histories, or that the chance of survival should be thrown open to competitive examination.

"Say, Harry," I said. "You know Sammy Hoggan well?"

Harry knew everybody. He nodded, very serious. He knew that whatever he said to me, whatever anyone said to me,

13

might mean life or death for someone. So it was a solemn business talking to me.

It had probably never crossed his mind that he might be one of the ten. When you really came down to it, there were a surprising number of people who took it for granted that they had no right to live, if only a few could survive.

"What's the matter with him?" I asked.

"Thought you knew. His girl left him."

"That all?"

"Son," said Harry seriously, "I've lived a bit longer than you, even if you're the most important man around just now. Never say, 'That all?' about someone's reasons for doing anything. That's only your reaction to the circumstances as you know them, and it means next to nothing."

"Okay," I said. "What was the girl like?"

"No good."

"Because she left Sammy?"

"That among other things. Sammy's a good boy, Bill. You'd like him. It's a pity you've no chance now of knowing what he's like."

Unexpectedly, Pat said something coarse and regrettably audible. One of the unfortunate things about Pat was that she could get completely drunk on a thimbleful of whisky.

One of the others, though it ill becomes me to say it, was that when people called her the unpleasant things people so often call beautiful, reckless girls, they were for once perfectly right.

2

After we'd had another drink or two I decided to go to Havinton, five miles over the hill. Pat wanted to come, but I liked her better sober. She got drunk easily and sobered easily. By the time I got back she'd be all right.

Something was going to happen that afternoon that I wasn't going to like. I had put it off as long as I could. For a while I had thought I was going to be able to put it off until it was too late.

When I first came to Simsville Father Clark came to see me. I'd been told that if I was to co-operate with anyone it should be with ministers of all faiths. We were pretty free; we had little or nothing to do with the police, and nothing at all with other local authorities. But the job the ministers were doing, strangely enough, linked up quite well with ours.

Father Clark was one of those people who are transparently sincere and so humble that you can't help being uncomfortable in their presence and glad to get away. When he said he and Pastor Munch and the Reverend John Mac-Lean would like to have a meeting with me as soon as possible and discuss a few things, I had been vague and managed to avoid fixing a date. There was a solemnity about working together with clergymen of three faiths that reminded me, when I didn't want to be reminded, that I wasn't just Bill Easson any more.

The three men of God were so busy that it was easy for me to keep stalling. Sure, I was shirking my responsibilities. My only excuse was that that was the only responsibility I was consciously shirking. Other lieutenants would have other things to square with their consciences. Men with color prejudices would have to face up to the idea that the catastrophe wasn't a special dispensation to remove all but pure whites from the human race; some lieutenants whose blood crawled at the thought would pick colored men to go to Mars, knowing that if they didn't they would never know peace again. Men who hadn't noticed children for years would realize that there was such a thing as responsibility to young people; the intelligent would discover responsibility for the stupid; and of course all of us were adjusting ourselves to the idea that a baby just out of the womb, a dreamy, clear-skinned boy of eight, a beautiful girl of seventeen, a man in the prime of life, and an old toothless woman were all units in the fantastic new numerology we were using.

Anyway, this responsibility had caught up with me. I was to see the three clergymen later that afternoon. Meantime I'd had enough of being important, so I went to Havinton. In Havinton I was just a man among men. The gods there were

16

Lieutenants Britten, Smith, Schutz, and Hallstead. From which it might be gathered that Havinton was about four times the size of Simsville.

It's difficult to say how much warning we had of the end of the world. The first concrete thing was certainly Professor Clubber's article in the *Astronomical Journal* two years earlier, in which he said that if and if and if, the sun was going to fry at least the four nearest planets to crisps very soon. But who reads the *Astronomical Journal?*

No, it was a year before the possible end of the world was publicized even enough for crackpot cults to spring up—and God knows that doesn't take much publicity.

The trouble was, at first it was more or less all-inclusive. Not only Earth but Mercury, Venus, Mars, and the asteroids as well. That was as far as any spaceship from Earth had gone so far. Someday someone would land on one of the satellites of the bigger worlds, but not in time to affect this problem. So at first there was no question of any refuge. No preparations were made—there was nothing to prepare for. And priceless months were wasted.

The sun wasn't going to become a nova, or anything like that. It was only going to burn a little brighter for a while, like an open fire suddenly collapsing on itself and shooting out spurts of flaming hydrogen. Astronomers on distant worlds, if there were any, would have to be advanced indeed before they would change Sol's brightness index as a result of any observations they might be making.

It was such a tiny change, astronomically speaking, which the sun was going to make that one could understand why cults like the Sunlovers started. The first I heard of this group, it was a thousand strong. When I checked on the figure it was three million. A week later there were over a hundred million members of an international Sunlovers' Association.

What the Sunlovers were going to do was just get used to the change before it came. They flowed to the tropics. They found the hottest spots on Earth. The SunA embraced sun bathing, primitivism, nudism, Egyptology, swimming, anything remotely connected with the sun. The SunAs, as they called themselves (pronounced Sunays), soon had a routine in which clothes were ceremoniously torn to pieces and the body was offered to the sun.

Well. But don't let's be hard on the SunAs. Fully ninety-five per cent of them were sane, sensible people—it was only the extremists who carried out those stunts like walking through fires and burning ice factories and giving birth to children out in the blazing sun and publicly branding their breasts with the SunA sign by sunrays focused through giant magnifying glasses.

Most of the SunAs were people who thought that if they took the step of converting their environment from, say, fur-clad Alaska to bathing-suited Bermuda they would have gone part of the way to being ready for the admittedly tiny increase in radiated solar energy. They didn't get up before dawn to pay their respects to the sun; or if they did, it was out of politeness, not to the Sun God, but to the more fervid SunAs around them.

What the SunAs couldn't or wouldn't understand was that astronomical temperatures, even solar-system temperatures, ranged from $-273°$ C. to $20,000°$ C., and humanity was only comfortable between $10°$ and $30°$. Certainly people could exist at below-zero and above-blood-heat temperatures. But while nobody wanted to claim accuracy to a degree or two, there was unquestionably going to be no place left on the surface of Earth where water would remain liquid. . . .

Then there were the Trogs, who weren't so much going to get used to the new conditions as run away from them. Basically, if the aim of all the Trog societies must be reduced to its simplest terms, they were going to dig holes in the ground. Oh, certainly some of the Trogs were scientists genuinely planning on survival in a $250°$–$500°$ C. world. They were working on a basis of shelter, to equalize temperatures; refrigeration, to convert the energy of heat to the task of keeping a few cubic feet cool; hydroponics, for food and water—all the obvious things. The only thing was, it was like trying to move a mountain with a wooden spade. It wasn't going to work. Undoubtedly some Trogs were going to live longer than anyone else when the heat really came on, but that was all—minutes, hours, or days. There just wasn't time to find out how to make a bubble which one could never leave in a 300° C. world and keep it at what had once been normal Earth temperature. Our science was a caveman technology—we knew about lighting fires and staying warm, but our only solution when there was too much heat was to go somewhere else.

Yes, it was a pity we worked on wrong premises for so long. Until well on in July there was still room for doubt; but then two things were shown conclusively. One was that life would cease on Earth on or about September 18; the other was that Mars, instead of sharing in the disaster, would almost certainly be more habitable after the solar change than before.

It was a double blow. Before that, people could refuse to believe that the world was in any danger. After it, there was the knowledge that *some* people would live. The law of survival became Mars at Any Price.

A few people who moved quickly enough actually gave themselves life simply by booking passages to Mars. But very soon the survival of the human race was organized. The planners and statisticians got to work. And about their deliberations and premises I know nothing.

The edict was that 1 in 324.7 people could go to Mars. That was pretty damn good, we were told. It could be achieved only by having every machine plant that could possibly be used for the job feverishly producing anything that could prise itself off Earth before it was too late.

Pretty damn good it might be, but it meant that 324 out of every 325 people all over Earth were going to die.

Somehow one person out of every three hundred or so had to be picked out for a chance to live on a strange world. And

19

the job had been given, rightly or wrongly, to the men who were actually to take them to their new home.

There wasn't much time for argument. Friday, September 18, was deadline. For a few hours after noon on Friday the real spaceships, the ships properly built before the heat was on, would be landing and taking away extra cargoes of human beings. But by noon Friday all the rush jobs, the lifeships made in desperate haste for one trip only, would have to be clear of Earth. Otherwise they might as well stay where they were.

So they sent us out—*us*, the men and women who happened to be able to handle a ship—to collect the ten people who would go with each of us.

See what I mean about needing a library for the whole story? The details of how agreement was reached on that point would make a book.

We weren't anything special, the newly appointed gods who had to pick ten people out of 3250 or so. It just so happened that the way to get most people off the Earth was to build thousands of tiny ships into which eleven people could be packed. A little more time, and perhaps mighty ships could have been built, and a different method of selection employed.

Anyone who had any hope of being able to handle a lifeship was given a command. I had been a radio officer on an expeditionary spaceship. At that I had a better background than some of the men and women who were going to try to take lifeships to Mars. Mary Horner, the stewardess on the exploration ship, had a command, I knew.

In the end, of course, the real shortage wasn't of lieutenants but of lifeships. Otherwise they'd have had training schools set up to turn out space pilots in a hurry (normally, it only took five years).

I had been given Simsville, which was just big enough to supply a lifeship complement and no more. I'd never been there before, of course. Lieutenants were invariably sent where they knew nobody.

And four days before takeoff, I had my list of people who were to live.

The Powells. They were Mr. and Mrs. America, Jr. Fred Mortenson, the brash, clean-limbed young hero-to-be. Harry Phillips, who wasn't quite sure it was right for people to go dashing away from the world that had given them life, merely because it was now going to bring them death. Little Bessie Phillips, who didn't know what it was all about (who did?). Miss Wallace, a schoolteacher and a good one. People like her would be needed. The Stowes, Mr. and Mrs. America, Sr., and Jim, their son. Leslie Darby.

Because Leslie was going, Pat would stay. Don't allow for what you think the rest of you are going to do, I'd been told, with all the other lieutenants of lifeships. But it was difficult to escape the idea that there would be plenty of young and beautiful girls on the list for Mars. So I had only one in my ten.

I had only three things to worry about now.

One: staying alive till I left Simsville. There were fanatics now; later there would be disappointed, angry, terrified people who would sink themselves in a mob.

Two: getting my ten away from Simsville. That wouldn't be easy, despite what I'd been told and the arrangements which had been made.

Three: getting my lifeship to Mars. But that, the most difficult and important, was the one which worried me least. That was me and an untested, hastily built ship against space. The others were me against my fellow men.

3

The three clergymen were met together at Father Clark's house when I arrived back in Simsville from my brief holiday in Havinton. As Father Clark ushered me in there was that uneasy silence that comes when a group's frank discussion of someone is interrupted by the arrival of the someone.

The Reverend John MacLean was heavy and blunt. "Let's waste no time, Lieutenant Easson," he said. "You probably think your time's valuable, and I know I think mine is. Will you start the ball rolling, or shall I?"

I sat down and tried to feel at home. "You, I think," I said. "Why do you want to see me, anyway?"

"First," said MacLean briskly, "let's get one thing cleared up. We don't expect——"

"I know. You don't expect to go, but . . . But what?"

"Isn't that a little unnecessary?" asked Father Clark gently. "I know you must have found it necessary to adopt a defensive, even a suspicious attitude, Lieutenant Easson, but——"

"Sorry," I said. "Trouble is, it seems years since I could talk to anyone in a straightforward way." I had a good look at them. Cynically I had half expected that they would be squabbling among themselves, but I could see no sign of that.

"That's part of our reason for wanting to talk to you," said Pastor Munch. He was one of those little men with astonishingly deep voices. The room seemed too small to contain his vibrating organ tones. One was inclined not to notice what he said, so fascinating was the sound of it. "You see," he went on, "the three of us here, Lieutenant Easson, feel we are responsible for Simsville. That is our success and our failure. We are not big enough to be responsible for the whole world. We must limit our sphere to be effective. I'm purposely not talking theology—my point is simply that anything that happens to the people of Simsville happens to us. And anything that is *going* to happen we must carefully examine and test and if necessary explain to our people."

"Exactly," said MacLean briskly. "You are an instrument of God. Sometimes the phrase has been used as an excuse. Instrument of a higher power. A shrug of the shoulders. Nothing can be done but accept."

He leaned forward and tapped firmly on the arm of my chair. "That attitude is apathy," he declared. "And apathy is anti-God. We feel, all three of us, that it is up to us to examine and test and if necessary explain, as my colleague says, this instrument of God. We can help or impede. Or we can guide."

23

MacLean's blunt though not unfriendly approach demanded frankness. "You mean," I said, "you can help or impede or guide *me*."

"There is no question," said Father Clark quickly, "of impeding."

Munch murmured assent, the rumble of a distant avalanche. MacLean said nothing, staring back at me.

"I didn't want this meeting," I admitted, "and I delayed it as long as I could. That was because I was prepared to promise nothing."

MacLean nodded. "You came with your mind made up, in fact," he said.

I nodded too. "Half made up, anyway."

Father Clark almost wrung his hands. He was too kindly to like this kind of plain speaking.

"What did you think," asked MacLean, "that we might ask you to promise?"

"To take all the saints," I said bluntly, "and leave the sinners."

I hadn't noticed Munch's eyes before. They were very soft, brown, very sincere. They met mine and I wasn't quite happy. "Of course you will take the saints," he said, "and leave the sinners. But you did not think, did you, that we should insist that only we knew the difference?"

"I shall take whom I like," I said flatly, "on the basis of my own conscience."

Pastor Munch nodded. "That is what I meant."

MacLean nodded too. "I don't think you've been thinking straight, young man," he told me. "On your main job, yes. Perhaps you have. On the part we would play, no. How could we possibly dictate to you in any way what you should do? It's a waste of time for us to decide what we would have done if things had been different. I've heard about you. I've seen you once or twice. I know you're going to do your best. Therefore you're the best possible instrument, and if I'd had anything to do with your selection I'd have chosen you."

I tried to swallow the lump in my throat, unreasonably

24

ashamed of it. Munch met my eyes again, and his own softened still more.

"We understood your burden," he told me, "but we weren't quite certain that you did. I am glad you do. You must realize its weight before it begins to lighten."

More was said, and I think there were handshakes and blessings and promises of any help I needed. But I don't want to go into that.

These three were not only priests of God; they were good men.

4

I stepped straight from peace into hell.

I had seen signs that made it plain there was going to be trouble in Havinton. For that matter there was going to be trouble everywhere. But in Simsville, with only three thousand population, I had thought I was lucky. A crowd in Simsville—even a mob, if it became that—could only contain three thousand people. A mob in Havinton could be thirteen thousand strong—and that's pretty strong.

But as I reached the town square on the way back to my hotel from Father Clark's house I found things could be pretty bad in Simsville too.

Our first riot was raging in the square. I stood and watched. I was safe, comparatively. No one but a madman was going to harm the one man who could give him life.

There was nothing to indicate the reason for the fight. Probably no one knew it. Frightened people are angry people; and if a man is angry enough, a remark that it might rain is enough to start a fight.

Watching it sickened me. If I'd had any real authority I'd have tried to stop it; but I was nothing, and nobody could stop it. I had no backing. The police were there in the fight— whether as police or just as contestants I didn't know.

I'd never seen a really dirty brawl. I'd never seen men throw children aside, drag women about by the hair, kick unconscious men in the ribs and stomach, and tear at each other with their nails. I didn't want to see it. I moved to go, and then realized it was still my job to pick ten people out of this rabble. It was part of my job to watch.

Brian Secker had a man I didn't know on the ground and was battering his head on the concrete. That was manslaughter, or very soon would be. Could I take a man I knew to be a killer to Mars? Secker came off the list of improbables and went on the list of impossibles. That was the only punishment I could inflict, and he would never know.

Harry Phillips was in the fight but not of it. He was ignoring mere brutality and doing what little he could to stop anything worse. That was no surprise. I knew Harry. His place on the lifeship was confirmed.

I could see Mortenson on the other side of the battle, but he was fighting with a smile on his lips. To him a fight meant fun, not terror or torture. He fought men his own size. My gaze passed on.

It was a shock to see Jack Powell battering Al Wayman to a pulp. But then I saw Marjory lying unconscious beside them, and turned elsewhere.

I started toward Pat. She was almost hidden by three men. But past her I saw Leslie, trapped in a corner with half a dozen children she had gathered behind her for safety. I went to her instead. The three round Pat were only tearing her clothes, and that was to be expected.

But when I reached Leslie she screamed and pushed me toward Pat.

"They won't hurt her," I said. "She's——"

"You fool!" Leslie shouted at me. "Look at them not hurting her. Naturally they'll hurt her—kill her if they can. Haven't you the sense to see that?"

I turned, and then Leslie didn't have to urge me. They were using Pat as a punchball. People who can't defend themselves any more can very soon be punched to death. Particularly women.

I couldn't drag them off. I could only go and show them I was there. They could have killed me. But the knowledge that their only chance of life depended on me sobered them, and they slunk away. Pat was on the ground, unconscious.

I picked her up and took her to Leslie. She was breathing. She would live, no doubt. The children behind Leslie stared.

Pat opened her eyes. "God, what hit me?" she gasped. Then she saw the gaping children behind us. "Turn your backs, kids," she said. "You're too young for this kind of show."

She was hurt less seriously than anyone would have thought.

Leslie pulled her dress over her head and helped me to get it on Pat. "That makes you Exhibit A in the peepshow, Leslie," Pat observed. "Never mind, my need is greater than thine."

The fight was suddenly, for no apparent reason, all but over. People disappeared like snowflakes in the sun.

That was our first fight, and very nearly the worst. People hadn't realized, till then, what could happen when such a fight started among men and women who had only four days to live. They hadn't known that they themselves would be ready to kill, and others to kill them.

Pat couldn't walk, but she was very easy to carry. It was

safe now to send the children home. They went with backward glances at us. Already, so little impression had the
fight made on them, curious little sniggers passed among
them.

As I picked Pat up, I half turned to Leslie, frowning. The
kids were giggling as if at a dirty joke, not quite understood.
Leslie was a schoolteacher, and perhaps precocious youngsters found prurient amusement in the sight of her dressed
like a lurid magazine cover. But I had heard those sniggers
before, when Leslie wasn't around.

She read my thoughts. "It's not me," she said with an
embarrassed grin that made Pat leer up at me. "It's you."

"Me?" Just in time I stopped myself twisting to see if
there was a hole in my pants or something.

"The schools were closed," said Leslie, "because it seemed
silly to keep them open. Because teachers couldn't be
bothered. Because parents wanted their children with them.
But we weren't allowed to tell the children why the schools
were closing."

"I know. Mad, of course—why try to keep it a secret that
the world's going to end on Friday?"

Leslie nodded. She was talking very quickly, trying to keep
my attention on what she was saying and off her body, I suppose. She needn't have been ashamed of it. It was slight by
most standards, but sweet.

"Yes, but don't you see?" she went on rapidly. "We're told
not to tell them, so they learn about it from each other, in
dark corners, as something shameful. Some parents, of course,
are wise, and explain simply. But others run away from the
problem and let their children learn the truth as a misty
horror . . ."

I could work out the rest for myself. It was foolish to try
to hide this new fact of life and death from children; but it
was no surprise that people tried it. They forgot, or didn't
realize, that while one could conceal facts from children one
could never conceal tension. And it centered in me.

I was taking Pat to my hotel, which was quite close. I

shrugged off the problem of the children—I couldn't carry everything. But I remembered something else which had aroused my curiosity even in the middle of the riot.

"What did you mean, Leslie," I asked, "when you said naturally they'd hurt Pat and hadn't I the sense to see that?"

Leslie went red as I looked at her, but it wasn't a blush of embarrassment this time. She said irritably, "Don't be a fool, Bill." She was right. I was a fool. I should have known.

I looked down at Pat. "You know what she's talking about?" I asked, more to get her mind off her bruises than anything else. But Pat didn't know, and said so.

"They knew Pat was sure of a place on the lifeship," Leslie said suddenly, bitterly. "Naturally they wanted to kill her. I can even see their point of view myself."

Pat tried to laugh, but gave it up. "Tell her, Bill," she said weakly.

But it was important that no one should know he was going to Mars, or not going. People could become desperate when they knew there wasn't any chance. Even Pat, despite what she said.

So I said noncommittally, "Nobody's sure of his or her place, Leslie. Until Thursday night, when eleven of us leave here, no one knows that he'll go or stay. You can see it must be like that if you only think about it for a minute."

Leslie frowned. We were in the lounge of my suite. I set Pat down on a sofa. "But . . ." Leslie said.

Pat really laughed this time. "Still don't believe it, Leslie?" she said mockingly. "Listen. Bill and I have never discussed this, except when I told him, right away, I didn't expect to be one of the ten. I don't say I want to die—who does? But if Bill won't tell you straight, I will. He wouldn't take a girl like me to Mars. If he did, he wouldn't be Bill. So I can just carry on being myself without trying to buy myself a place on the ship by being someone else. See?"

Leslie nodded, incredulously. "I'll go and call the doctor," she said. I threw out a shirt and a pair of slacks for her, without out a word.

"I'd think more of her if she believed you," I said, frowning, when she had gone.

"Can you expect her to?" Pat asked wryly. "We're always together. We . . ."

But she found talking not worth the effort, and stopped.

I thought Pat had come out of the affair better than Leslie, and the frown didn't come off my face. You could judge people by what they believed of others. Was I making a mistake?

Or was Pat, after all, putting up a magnificent bluff, for the highest stakes of all?

5

I had a caller next morning before I was properly awake.
Pat, as I had suspected, was tough. She was up and moving
about, in a green silk dressing gown of mine, ordering breakfast, and introducing the famous feminine touch to the suite.

She had stayed in the apartment. There was nothing in
that. If desperate people wanted to kill her and only I could
protect her, it was obvious that she should stay with me. But
when I heard the knock I nodded toward the bathroom.

She shook her head definitely. "It's probably only Leslie,"
she said, without lowering her voice. "Besides, the less openly

32

a thing's done, the more weight people give it. A whiff of my perfume—and I use very strong perfume, haven't you noticed?—no sign of me, and it would be settled beyond doubt. Everyone would know you were taking me along."

The truth of the matter was, she just didn't want to hide. She had crossed to the door as she spoke, and opened it.

It was Mortenson. The door hid him for a second or two, so I didn't see his reaction when Pat opened the door to him. By the time he was inside he was taking her presence for granted. Mortenson was never discomposed by anything.

"Say, Bill," he said in his easy, friendly manner. "After what happened yesterday, don't you think you could use some help? I mean, you're all on your own here. Pat doesn't count when the broken glass starts flying. Suppose I move in with you?"

I considered it. There might be times when I'd be glad of Mortenson around. But I knew I was right in having as little as possible to do with the people I had already chosen. The case of Pat proved it, though I hadn't chosen her. Everyone about me was suspect. I didn't want Mortenson, the Powells, Leslie, and Harry Phillips to be found in an alley with knives in their backs.

"Smart, Fred," Pat remarked admiringly. "Just in case Bill hasn't had a chance to appreciate your sterling qualities, you want to hang around and give him the opportunity. You needn't worry. He knows what a great guy you are."

He admitted his motive without a trace of irritation. Mortenson was always easy, friendly, natural. "The thought had crossed my mind," he said. "How about it, Bill?"

"Better not," I said, and explained why, without telling him he was on the list. He nodded. "Reasonable," he admitted. "More than that, you're perfectly right. Announce the names of the ten people who're going with you, and it's the National Bank to one peanut not more than one of your ten would be alive the same night. Say, Pat, if Bill won't take my offer—when you want to go out and Bill isn't around, give me a ring, will you? I don't pretend I'm crazy about you, but

I'd hate to see you after that swan-white neck of yours had had an interview with a meat ax."

Pat shuddered. "You put things so realistically," she said.

Before he went Mortenson warned me that he wouldn't be the last caller I had that morning. "I came early to get in first," he said frankly. "I know Miss Wallace is coming to see you, and the Powells, and Sammy Hoggan——"

"Sammy!" I exclaimed. "Can he walk?"

"I knew you'd underrate Sammy," said Mortenson, shaking his head. "Nearly twenty-four hours ago he went out flat. Now, apart from a head he'd be glad to sell if anyone would buy it, he's the old Sammy. Suddenly realized the girl wasn't worth it."

Knowing he couldn't leave a better impression by staying longer, he went out and closed the door quietly.

Mortenson was a puzzle—which meant, of course, that I didn't quite understand him. I can't hope to convey the principal thing about him when you met him—the impression he gave of being larger than life, of having done and seen everything. He was the man of ten talents. After he had gone one wondered what was so startling about what he had said and done; but one never wondered that at the time.

I looked at Pat quizzically. "You don't like him," I said.

"On the contrary," she retorted flippantly, "I've been in love with him for years. Now and then he's even acknowledged it in passing."

"You don't sound as if you loved him."

"Think hard, Bill. Can you imagine me sounding as if I were in love with anybody?"

That rang the bell. Pat had grown up in a school of life in which the first rule to be learned was: Show your feelings, and someone will slap you down for it.

"You wouldn't like to tell me about it, would you?" I asked.

"There's nothing to tell. What does a lady tell a gentleman about another gentleman?" She was very bitter over the words "lady" and "gentleman." I said nothing, hoping she would fill the silence with words. Presently she did.

"I threw myself at him," she said. "I didn't know any better. But it didn't matter, for he was kind and understanding. He caught me and put me down gently. That's all you can ask of anyone, isn't it? This was when I was seventeen. I tried again, and this time he didn't put me down gently. He held me for quite a while, and when he did put me down it wasn't exactly gentle. By this time he was a little bored with me. I was demanding, you see."

I could hardly imagine Pat being demanding. But maybe I was hearing about a different Pat. Most of us are a lot of different people in the course of our lives.

"Don't blame him," she went on. "Whatever you do, don't blame Fred. That would be unjust." I didn't know whether the irony in her voice was applicable to what she was saying at the time, or just to her life. Her whole life, I thought. "After all, did *you* duck? Well, the same thing went on happening over and over again. Exactly the same thing. Fred and I meet, as if for the first time, and play the same old broken record."

"Why?" I asked bluntly.

"Easy," she said lightly. "Because that's the nearest I can get to being happy. And because Fred isn't made of asbestos."

She had said all she was going to say on the subject, but I didn't need any more. It was one of those stories that begin: "Things would have been so different if . . ." Maybe they would; what always seems to me to matter is what things are, not what they might have been. But I couldn't help breaking my own rule and wondering if things would have been different if Pat and Sammy had got together, as they obviously never had.

"How come you didn't know about this girl of Sammy's?" I asked.

She shrugged. "Never had much to do with Sammy. He and I started off on the wrong foot a long time ago, I guess." She gave a hard laugh. "It happens with the nicest people sometimes."

35

We had just finished breakfast when the Powells arrived. They weren't in the least surprised to see Pat, but her presence seemed to bother them. So after a while she went into the back bedroom.

The Powells still had trouble coming to the point. I hoped they weren't going to break down and beg me to take them to Mars because Marjory was going to have a baby, or for any other second-feature reason.

It was Marjory who managed to tell me the reason for their visit at last, though not without more hedging. She was polishing her fingernails very carefully, stopping now and then to pull her perfectly straight skirt straight. "We didn't want to say anything about it," she said, "because we didn't think it would matter anyway, but all the same we felt we ought to—you understand, don't you? Just in case. It's only fair."

I waited, knowing that anything I said would only be an excuse for more circumlocution—they would explain in great detail that they didn't mean *that*.

"I said there wasn't any chance of your picking us," said Marjory, "but Jack said after all, you might. So we thought we'd better tell you not to. Not that it was likely, but——"

"Why?" I asked bluntly. "You mean you want to die?"

"I mean I can't help it," said Marjory simply. "I'm too great a risk, Bill. I had a miscarriage once and the doctor told me another pregnancy would kill the child and me."

"You think only people who can have children should go?"

"It's more than that, Bill. It didn't seem to matter . . . I'm pregnant now."

"I see," I said.

"Of course you may think we had our nerve thinking you were going to pick us out," said Marjory quickly. "It's not that. It's just that you had to know, in case."

There was nothing for me to say. Could I tell them they had been on the list? Obviously not. Would it make them feel any better if I said they'd never been seriously considered? No. I could only murmur stupidly that I was sorry. It wasn't what I had expected, but it was still second-feature stuff.

Pat came back as soon as the Powells had gone. I told her about them and went on, "I wonder why everybody's chosen this morning to come and tell me these things?"

"Easy enough," Pat replied. "Five people died in the fight yesterday. Twenty-four more went to the hospital. Six were sent to the county jail, to come up in court next Monday. Only there probably isn't going to be a next Monday, so they won't see anything more in their lives but their cells. People suddenly realize that this isn't just a nightmare that will be over tomorrow morning. This is Tuesday. If they haven't convinced you by Thursday night that you ought to take them to Mars, they're going to die."

I was more interested in Pat than in what she said. I remembered that there were now two vacancies for Mars. There was no argument with what Marjory had said. I couldn't give one of those priceless places on my lifeship to someone who might die in a few months or, worse still, become on Mars an invalid who would have to be looked after.

I didn't want to see anyone else. I wanted to sit down and think. But the procession went on.

Miss Wallace had early lost all sign of youth and become ageless. I knew she was only thirty, but she could have passed for forty-five or fifty, if she set her mind to it.

The reason for her visit was to make a plea that Leslie Darby should go.

"You may think she's young and frivolous," said Miss Wallace earnestly (quite unnecessarily, for Leslie was obviously young and no one but Miss Wallace would have thought her frivolous), "but if you haven't seen her with children, take my word for it, she has a very special gift. That will be needed in a new world. Sometimes I'm afraid, Lieutenant Easson—I hope you don't think this is presumptuous—that you and other young men like you will build up a Spartan colony—hard, brave men and women with no time for the softer things of life. Perhaps that is right. Only I feel that the children in such a world will grow up harder and braver still, and a new race will be born that will be cruel and ignorant and——"

"I don't think any of us want that, Miss Wallace," I told her. I got rid of her soon afterward, for after all she was wasting her time and mine. Leslie was going. So was Miss Wallace, though she seemed to have no thought of that. Besides, I had an uncomfortable feeling her sincerity would weaken me and make me say something I might regret.

"Let's go out," said Pat. "Otherwise everybody in Simsville will come."

"Well, don't you think I ought to see them?"

"You're not their pastor."

"No, but I can give them life in the hereafter."

"That's almost blasphemous," said Pat. It surprised me. I wouldn't have credited her with a clear idea of what blasphemy was, and I'd certainly never have thought she'd be concerned about it.

"Anyway, I'd like to know what's bothering Sammy," I said. "I'm curious to see him sober. I wonder what he wants."

Pat grunted cynically. "He wants a chance to see Mars, of course," she said. "Now that he's wakened up in a world in which he has only three days to live, he's coming to crawl on his belly in front of you."

I didn't like her to speak like that. One moment she had me on the point of giving her Marjory Powell's place. The next she confirmed my belief that that would be a mistake.

Perhaps I took my job too seriously. Perhaps I thought I really was a god.

6

I'd never have guessed in a hundred years why Sammy Hoggan wanted to see me. What had happened to him often happens to people after a hard drinking bout. Suddenly it is all over, they feel like hell, but their brains are ice-cold and emotionless. I've known scientists in such circumstances to come up suddenly, disinterestedly, with the answer to problems that had been bothering them for years.

He came in, walking carefully, as if his head was balanced on a single pin. He was a different Sammy. He looked at me, then at Pat, then back at me.

"I wonder if I should say what I came to say," he murmured.

"Let's hear it."

"Maybe I should keep it to myself, since it doesn't seem to have occurred to anyone else. But it's a disturbing thought, and you might be able to settle it for me. If you can't, I think I'll go back to the rye, for another reason."

"Everybody's evasive," I complained. "Spit it out."

"Can I ask you a few questions?" He lowered himself carefully into a chair. "How long does it take to build a regular spaceship?"

"Nearly a year."

"How many people could the regular ships have taken off while there's still time?"

"I don't know. A few hundred. About one in five million people. What are you getting at?"

"Where's your lifeship being built? Have you seen it?"

It should have been obvious what he was thinking, but I didn't see it. Pat did. She caught her breath and looked at Sammy with horror.

"At Detroit. With thousands of others. The whole place has been evacuated and made into a military reservation. Like Philadelphia and Phoenix and Birmingham and Berlin and Omsk and Adelaide. But you know about that. Yes, I've seen the lifeships. They won't be ready until a few hours before takeoff. No trials. Plenty of them won't get near Mars. Is that what you mean? It's not publicized, but anyone who knows the first thing about interplanetary flight can work that out for himself. So?"

"Suppose only one in five million people had a chance of life. What would have happened on Earth?"

"It's not a pleasant thought," I admitted. "That riot yesterday was nothing to what we'd have had, all day and every day, all over the world. But human beings are pretty ingenious when the heat's on. It didn't take long to draw up plans for ships that could be made in eight weeks, when it was really necessary. So what you're visualizing didn't happen."

40

"Yes," said Sammy quietly. "It didn't happen. Because, as you say, human beings can be pretty ingenious."

I saw at last what he meant, and laughed. He had had me worried.

"You mean that knowing what would happen if only one in five million people could be taken to safety, the high-ups instituted a hoax, to keep the world quiet," I said. "One in three hundred is different. It's an appreciable chance. People won't throw it away. They'll be very careful until they know they've lost it. That's it, isn't it?"

I laughed again. "If there were any real point in it," I went on, "I might begin to believe it. But where's the gain? What would it matter if people all over the world fought and pillaged and looted and murdered? It'll all be the same when the mercury shoots out of the top of all the thermometers."

"There might even be a point," said Sammy. "Who's going in the regular ships? Groups carefully selected—not by *pro tem* lieutenants whose only qualification is that they know one end of a spaceship from the other. The real ships are taking the essential people, the equipment, the supplies——"

"Naturally, when the lifeships are such a gamble."

"More natural still if none of the lifeships are expected to arrive. Perhaps not even to leave Earth. Don't you see what I'm afraid of? The high-up officials knew that if they told the truth everything would be chaos. Mobs would destroy the ships that wouldn't take them to Mars. They'd kill anyone suspected of being chosen to go. When a ship landed, anywhere, a million people would be swarming around it before the ports opened.

"Now see the way it is. The top officials of all governments can carefully, quietly select the people for the colonies, take them to the spaceports, and get them aboard the ships. There may be incidents, but people don't go wild for fear they might lose their chance of a place on a lifeship. See what a smart, hellish scheme it is? The people who are really going to Mars can prepare quietly, without being disturbed, while a third of the population of Earth is occupied building useless lifeships, and the other two thirds are busy behaving themselves and trying to catch some tinpot lieutenant's eye."

Pat was worried. I felt a great respect for her and Sammy. I knew—I didn't know how, but I knew they were concerned, not for themselves, for neither expected to go to Mars, but for the duped millions who thought they had a chance when (according to Sammy's theory) they had none.

No use to point out that even if it were true there might be something to be said for that method of ensuring that as many as possible of the right people should be taken to the new colony. Pat and Sammy were overcome by the horror of a world kept quiet by a cruel lie. I couldn't see it quite the same way, though it concerned me more than them.

I put my arm around Pat's shoulders.

"I won't argue with your theory, Sammy," I said, "though I could. I'll just say this. When you got that idea—had you ever been lower in your life? Weren't you miserable, in despair, half dead? Would you admit anything but the blackest, gloomiest thoughts?"

He grinned wryly. "You may have something there."

"Then suppose you get yourself feeling a little happier about things, and then have another look at this idea. It may look a little different."

"Pat wasn't feeling low," Sammy retorted. "And she seems to think there might be something in it."

"Pat thinks there's something in everything. On the surface she refuses to believe anything. But that often hides romanticism and imagination. And who said she isn't feeling low? She thinks she's made a mess of her life. She thinks she has no right to go to Mars. She wishes——"

Pat jammed her hand against my mouth, hard. I caught her wrists and scuffled mildly with her. She seemed to feel better after that.

Even Sammy almost smiled.

7

While Sammy was still with us the phone rang. Pat took it. She seemed determined that everyone should know she was with me—though what good that would do her I couldn't see. Quite the reverse. But people who set a lot of store on being honest and outspoken are often honest and outspoken when it does no good and a lot of harm.

The call was for Pat. She listened, slammed down the phone, and turned to us angrily. "Well, what do you know about that!"

"Nothing," said Sammy patiently, "until you tell us."

"That was my aunt. Somebody got into my room last night and destroyed everything—clothes, books, furniture, letters. The whole shooting match. Imagine anyone doing a thing like that!"

Sammy took the practical view. "Their usefulness has only been shortened by a day or two, anyway," he remarked. "Why should you care?"

"But——"

"It's just spite," I said. "Why be surprised, Pat? You're cynical about so many things—it should be no shock that when people hate you they take any small revenge they can."

Pat grinned involuntarily. "No, it isn't really," she admitted. "And as Sammy says, it hardly matters now. But it's pretty petty, isn't it?"

"What an odd juxtaposition," Sammy murmured. "Pretty petty. Pretty petty. Pretty petty."

Pat said she was going over to have a look around. I offered to take her, but surprisingly Sammy stood up and said he'd go with her. He put it neatly, using precisely the words that made any other arrangement impossible. In fact he cut me out. He must have been feeling a whole lot better than when he came in and talked despondency.

There was a knock on the door so soon after they had gone that I thought they had come back. I threw the door open casually, so sure it was Pat and Sammy that anyone else would have surprised me.

But I certainly didn't expect the melodrama of three masked men who brushed past me and shut the door.

I wasn't perturbed. Nothing could happen to me. I wouldn't have been so sure of one stranger, for individuals can be mad enough to kill the only man who can save them. But three— they couldn't be as mad as that, in the same way, all at once.

"Now what?" I asked. "More particularly, why?"

They all carried guns. The leader drew his and gestured with it, like a schoolboy.

"We mean to go to Mars, Easson," he said, his voice deliberately muffled. "If you get that clear for a start, we'll understand each other better."

"Then you'd better get out before I recognize any of you," I told them. "Otherwise it's very sure none of you will."

"One of us is going to stick beside you until takeoff. We figure that'll make a difference. We——"

His talking like a cowboy irritated me. For all I knew they might be kids playing a game.

"Get to hell out of here," I told them, "before I tear your masks off. What kind of a fool do you think I am?"

Nobody moved. So I explained the obvious. "If I die, *nobody* from Simsville goes to Mars," I said, a little more patiently. "They won't send another lieutenant now. So that won't help you. If you stick beside me as you say, it can only last until we get to Detroit, and then we'll be split. You won't be able to do anything about that. Then I can have you thrown into a cell somewhere and that's that. If you get me to promise anything—which would be very easy, for I'll say anything you like—it will last only till I know I'm safe. Then the program's as before. Is that clear?"

I looked from one to another of them. "Okay," I said. "You know where the door is. You just came in."

They went. As easily as that. I gave them credit for having realized before they came that that was probably what would happen. I couldn't really blame them for trying. I might have been weak enough and stupid enough to fall in with their plans. But it was a poor effort.

I'd had enough of my room. I went out to go to Henessy's. I saw the Stowes out with Jim and waved to them. They waved back tentatively. They belonged to the small group who still cared a great deal about what people would think. They didn't want anyone to say they were fawning on me, begging for what everyone wanted.

I saw Betty Glessor and Morgan Smith, who haven't been mentioned so far because I never thought of them. I had exchanged about ten words with them. But they were next on the list to the Powells.

45

That's what it came to in the end. The more I learned about people, the more likely they were to come off my list. Perhaps Smith was a drinker and a doper and a sadist and a killer—I hadn't time to find out. I didn't know he was any of these things, so I could take him to Mars.

Tentatively I scratched out the Powells and marked in Smith and Glessor.

Still looking after them, I almost ran into Leslie. She had no job, now that school was closed. She grinned. I stopped, having nothing to say, but no reason to walk past her when she seemed to want to talk.

"What are you doing?" she asked—a silly question if ever I heard one.

"Just killing time," I said.

"Like me to help you?"

"If you have any bright ideas."

She knew a little place down the valley I hadn't had a chance to see. She said it was a good place to think of when remembering Earth.

It was curious, I'd never thought of that. Perhaps because I'd lived in three country districts and four cities before I was ten, I had never felt any duty to any one place. I hadn't thought much about leaving Earth forever. I had realized vaguely that Harry Phillips would do so with a pang; but if everybody left on Earth was going to die, I was going to leave it without any regrets. What was Earth, anyway? Just a place. Define planets generically, and you had Mars and no loss on the deal that technology couldn't make up in a hundred years or so.

But as Leslie spoke I understood that no other planet would ever be made the same as Earth.

We stopped about two miles from Simsville, and there was no sign anywhere of mankind. Two hills folded in on us, hills thickly wooded. A stream meandered one way, then the other, in its search for lower ground. The clouds were very white and still against an almost tropical blue sky.

I found for the first time that though I had no eye for

46

beauty I could let it sink in and something in me appreciated it.

Leslie was wearing a watered-silk blue dress, and I could appreciate that too. It darkened her fair hair. I had always liked blue and gold.

"I wish . . ." said Leslie.

We had sat down in the shade, and she was leaning forward, her legs drawn up in front of her, pulling at her ankles.

"What do you wish?" I asked obligingly.

She seemed to have forgotten. "Why was it done like this?" she demanded.

I was disappointed. I had hoped I was getting away from Simsville and my job and its responsibility.

"How can one person get to know over three thousand people in fourteen days?" she went on. "You know you can't. You haven't tried. Oh, I don't say you aren't conscientious. I think you are. If you could have arranged the method of selection, all over the world, how would you have done it?"

I shrugged. "Phone book, I guess."

"How do you mean?"

"Every three hundred and twenty-fifth name."

Leslie caught her breath as if I'd suggested setting fire to a cathedral. "You *couldn't!*" she exclaimed. "That would be horribly callous."

"Why? It would be fair."

"But this way . . . at least there's a chance. The good, the wise, the clever, the beautiful *may* come through . . ."

"For God's sake!" I ejaculated, shocked by her lack of understanding. "Do you think that's what we're supposed to do? Take all the crowned heads in our thousands of little arks and ignore the rabble? Intellectual or artistic snobbery is no better than social snobbery. If I had Beethoven and Michelangelo and Napoleon and Madame Curie and Shakespeare and Helen of Troy and St. Peter here in Simsville, do you think I'd pick them?"

"Wouldn't you?" She had lost her horror, and in its place was a vast surprise.

"Suppose I did, what would happen to John Doe? Sure, if Simsville had a genius, I'd consider him. There aren't too many geniuses. But when it's one out of three hundred, we're not going to blot out the average man and woman by taking only the people who would come out at the head of a competitive examination in something or other. I . . ."

I didn't have the eloquence I needed. I knew I was right. I wanted her to see it. But how could I tell her that outstanding people, after all, were only clever dogs that had learned new tricks, and that John Smith was worth quite as much to himself as Shakespeare?

"Let's talk of something else," I said helplessly. "Or better still, not talk at all."

She nodded, hesitated, and then with sudden resolution put her hand to her throat.

Perhaps I was to blame as much as she was. I watched stupidly as she did things to her dress, and then became angry when there was no reason to be. After all, what was wrong in wanting to live? Why shouldn't people try anything and everything?

I knew too much about her, and not enough. If it had been Pat . . . well, if it had been Pat it would have been quite different. All I knew was that Leslie wasn't the kind to give herself casually to a near stranger. And that, instead of improving things, made them worse.

"You brought me here for this?" I asked furiously.

"Suppose I did?" she said defiantly.

I was wildly, unreasonably angry. I was also, quite irrationally, disappointed. "You think you could buy any lieutenant that way?" I demanded. "We could all of us have screen stars and princesses and models every night, no obligation, without having to bother about small-town teachers. What I should do is take you, and strike you off the list."

She became very still. It was all melodramatic, cheap, and stupid. She had been very clumsy in her effort to seduce me, not knowing how it was done. If she had known how to pretend to be in love with me, or at least attracted by me, the

48

cheapness would have gone. But only someone who was ashamed of herself could make the horrible mess Leslie made of it.

"Hadn't you even the sense to see," I said bitterly, "that any of us could have any woman we wanted? Don't you think I've had enough silly offers and proposals? People who promise to do everything I say on Mars, who offer me the equivalent of ten years' salary in whatever currency we use out there, if they have to sweat for twenty years to pay it . . . men who contract to do my killing for me in the colony, help me to set up a state of my own. Damn it, Leslie, isn't it obvious that I must have decided long ago on the only possible thing to do about such proposals—and that's to leave the people who make them behind?"

"You said . . . something that implied you'd picked me to go."

"Yes, I had."

Her head came up sharply and she laughed in my face. "I heard the same thing often when I was a child," she retorted. " 'I was going to give you something, but now I won't.' We all said it. It . . ."

I lunged away from her, back to Simsville. The blue silk dress still lay about her as if she were sitting in a sparkling pool.

8

It was hours, not days now. Very soon the ten who were going with me would be told. Whether they ever reached Mars would depend, among other things, on how well they could conceal their knowledge.

There was another fight in the square. I saw it from my window this time, keeping well hidden, for I didn't want it too definitely known where I was. Nobody wanted to fight, but nobody could help it. Everybody in the town was going to die, except eleven. The temperatures all over Earth were still normal, and the sun looked the same. It seemed incredible that there was nothing to see, hear, or feel.

I looked down from the sun to the square just in time to see Jack Powell die. Someone got him down and crushed his neck with his boot. With a sick feeling I saw it was Mortenson. Mortenson! In that moment something clicked into place and I began to understand Mortenson.

Favored. Fortunate. Strong, good-looking, healthy. He had so many things, how could he help but have everything he wanted? Like the beautiful girl who told him, in effect, and went on telling him, "Do what you like with me—I love you." People would forgive him for anything. Men liked him, women loved him.

He had hurt Pat. I had known that, but hadn't made any real effort to understand it. She had only talked once about her relations with Mortenson. Of course he had hurt Pat. She had asked for it—the whole world asked for it. Everybody was ready with forgiveness, eager to pardon the magnificent Mortenson.

In four words: he had too much. He had more than he could handle. Overnurtured, he had gone bad.

I didn't care about the rights and wrongs of the fight, or what had led to Mortenson's snuffing out Jack Powell's life. I would always remember the picture of Mortenson stamping on a man's neck, howling with joy. Mortenson was finished, as far as I was concerned.

Now Marjory would die alone, in sorrow and fear and hate. I would never see her again.

Betty and Morgan appeared, saw what was going on, and ran off down a side street. That was good. They hadn't compelled me to strike them off the passenger list of my lifeship. Sammy was there. He had a gun. Could he have been one of the three masked men? No—they were fools, and Sammy was no fool. Besides, he had been with Pat. Where was Pat?

I must have said it aloud, for she spoke behind me. "Come away from the window, Bill," she said. "It's like dope. It gets you in the end. You're not tough enough."

I brushed my hand over my eyes. She was right; I didn't

really know what was going on. At least, I recorded it faithfully enough, but it didn't mean to me what it should have meant.

The list was complete. Mortenson out, the Powells out, Leslie out. She had done something, I forgot what it was, but I remembered that she was off the list. Miss Wallace, Harry Phillips, Bessie Phillips, the Stowes, Jim Stowe, Betty Glessor, Morgan Smith. But that was only eight. Oh yes, Sammy and Pat.

"Pat," I said. "Did I ever tell you? You're going to Mars."

She wasn't surprised, as I had half thought, and she certainly wasn't delighted. She was very calm and serious.

"You really mean that?" she said.

"Of course. I wouldn't joke about it."

"No. That's what I thought. It's not just that you . . ."

I didn't know what she meant, and probably she didn't either. "It's not just anything," I said. "Of the population of Simsville, I don't know anyone who has more right to live than you."

I hoped it was taken as calmly in each case. I wouldn't know. I wasn't going to tell any of them myself, except Sammy and Pat.

The fight seemed to have stopped, or at least moved somewhere else. There were no shouts or screams as I waited, wondering how the other eight were taking it.

Pastor Munch was visiting the Stowes. That, of course, was the way. I couldn't visit the people I had chosen, I couldn't write or phone or telegraph, and I couldn't send anyone who had been close to me. The three clergymen had offered to help, and this was the way in which they could. No one would interfere with them as they went about visiting people; and I had not been in touch with them often enough or publicly enough for anyone to guess that they were my messengers.

Munch only knew about the Stowes. He hadn't wished to know more.

Father Clark was taking care of Harry Phillips. Harry would be incredulous, I guessed. I had thought all along that, left to himself, he would refuse. But mention of Bessie would shut him up. He would be afraid that if he said anything about himself Bessie might lose her chance.

Miss Wallace was another who might be dumfounded. Father Clark would tell her too.

I didn't know how Betty Glessor and Morgan Smith would react when MacLean told them they were going. They were the gamble of the group. But when it came to couples, one had to gamble. It seemed unfair to give half the available places to one family, but families wouldn't be split. That meant either couples who hadn't started to have their children, like Betty and Smith, or couples with only one child, like the Stowes.

There would be plenty of children on Mars. There always were when life for a group began anew. I would marry, naturally. I looked at Pat.

"Can you tell me now who else is going?" she asked. I told her.

"You've done a good job," she said.

I was inordinately relieved. Pat would know. So I had picked on roughly the right people.

"But . . ." she said, suddenly frowning.

"But what?"

"What about Leslie?" she demanded.

"I always meant to take a cross section. It was always you or Leslie. Not both."

Now she did look surprised. "But why me?"

"Pat, you always had a low opinion of yourself. You were quite right. You're nothing to write home about. Except maybe for your looks. But the sad thing is, other people rate even lower than you. So you go."

"Lower than me?" she murmured, in strange humility. "That's a pity."

The commonplace nature of her comment seemed the

funniest thing I had heard for months. I was close to hysteria, and I laughed until I was sore. A pity that people were such heels. A pity that the sun was going to radiate just the fraction more heat that meant the end of all life. A pity that only ten people from Simsville had a chance of life.

Sammy came in. I took control of myself.

"Glad to see you, Sammy," I said. "You're elected. You're going to Mars."

He nodded. He was another who wasn't surprised. "I thought that might happen," he admitted, "now Mortenson's dead."

"Dead?" I exclaimed.

"You didn't know? I thought you'd be watching from the window."

"Who killed him?"

"I did. If you didn't see what he was doing at the time, please don't ask me to describe it. I always had a weak stomach. And Pat?"

"She goes too."

He nodded again. But he was still thinking of Mortenson. "You wouldn't think that even something like this could change people so completely so quickly," he said.

Pat laughed, unaffectedly this time. "You should know better than that, Sammy," she said. "People don't change. Never. They may be changed, or they may reveal themselves, or we may have seen them wrong the first time. That's all."

"Never mind that," I said. "There isn't much time. Listen. You may have heard a rumor that a plane will pick up the selected people at the park."

Sammy nodded. "Well, there will be a plane," I said, "but that's only a blind. The plane is the escort for a helicopter that'll land here in the square about the same time. Everybody should be at the park. The people who mean to make trouble, anyway. The other eight who are going with us will know by now. They just have to get to the square, that's all. They should be safe so long as they don't give themselves away."

54

Sammy began to make objections, but I waved them aside rather petulantly. "Don't you think I've had time to see what's wrong with the plan in the last few weeks? It isn't mine. Anyway, what else could have been done? Nobody has more than a few hundred yards to go anyway, except the Stowes, and they'll come in their car. I know . . ."

Faintly but clearly we heard a plane.

"It's early," said Sammy.

"No. It's got to fly about and circle so that everyone believes it's the plane they've heard about, and they've only got to see where it lands—in the park or anywhere else. There's going to be no trouble, Sammy, unless too many people are smart and realize they're being fooled."

"But they've got a pretty good idea where you are."

"That was always the difficulty. We can't do anything about that—only hope the plane will be a greater attraction."

For long, tense minutes we waited. Then—because there had to be a little time in reserve—I got up. "Come on," I said.

The hotel had had no staff for a long time. The manager had no imagination at all, and he clung grimly to his job and his duties. There were no unauthorized people in the hotel.

We got down to ground level without seeing anyone. Naturally no one would come into the hotel, where they might miss us, when they only had to watch the exits.

The plane was still circling. Once or twice we heard it swoop to land, then climb again. The pilots of those planes had a big job. They had to be psychologists as well as heroes —for, of course, theirs was liable to be a suicide job. Mobs wherever this plan was adopted would tear these pilots to pieces when they learned they were just decoys.

The point was, the people were pretty certain I was at the hotel. Would anything make them leave? Only the conviction that I had somehow eluded them. All I could do about that I had done—have flares lit at the pavilion, flares that

55

would be visible anywhere in Simsville, and would surely make people think that I was at the park, signaling to the plane. The suspense was the cruelest, most effective part of it. People who at first had been grimly determined to wait in the square in the belief that I must appear there must have felt that belief waver and diminish as the plane swooped and flares lit the sky and people hurried past on their way to the park. The grim watchers must have panicked at the thought: *Some of these people must be going to Mars. And here we are watching them go!*

We heard the plane actually land. That, I thought, must break the last resistance of anyone who must now guess he had no chance of life on Mars.

We stepped boldly into the square. It was getting dark— deceptively dark. Even we, expecting it, didn't see the helicopter until it dropped in the square.

There were bodies in the square. It settled among them. I saw Mortenson lying outstretched, his hand straining for a gun he had never reached. He might have lived fifty years more, on another world.

Then shadows moved. We rushed for the helicopter, and I saw Harry Phillips carrying Bessie in his arms, Betty and Morgan running hand in hand.

Then Pat screamed.

Whether Mortenson had been all but dead or merely stunned didn't matter. He wasn't dead, and he had the gun. I saw Sammy go for his to make another try, and knew he would be just too late. Mortenson knew the time he had, and took careful aim. He could have had any of us—Sammy, who had shot him; or me, without whom no one from Simsville would live, and all would be brought down with Mortenson, who couldn't go himself.

But he chose Pat. Something in his twisted mind made him go for the girl who had loved him.

Mortenson and Pat died together. They were both good, clean shots. There were no last-breath speeches. Pat fell and Mortenson lay still.

I can't explain what I did. I never thought of Pat at all. I merely worked out that Leslie wouldn't be watching the plane, but at home, and I darted across to a phone booth. I dialed and got her at once. "The square, quick," I said, and slammed the phone down. That was all.

9

We didn't see much at Detroit. The organization was magnificent. The whole area was a vast clearing house, the few people who were running things there handling us like so many cans of beans. We had no gear; someone else was looking after that. There was a supply organization which took care of not only the essentials, like the problem of how we were going to live on Mars, but also the comparative luxuries, like how much of our literature and history and art we could afford to take along. But that wasn't our affair.

We got to Detroit late on Thursday night, were given a

meal, and swept into cots, all in the same room. We were then cheerfully informed that our meal had been drugged. We saw only two people. Two who would handle . . . how many lifeships' complements? Presumably the people who were keeping things running at Detroit would be collected later by a regular ship.

We slept until eleven in the morning—Friday morning. When we awoke, the world was still the same. We all wondered—I expect everyone did who looked at the sun that morning—whether the whole thing wasn't a mistake after all and life wouldn't go on the same as ever. But the fact was, of course, that we were approaching the last second that scientists *knew* was safe. Nothing would happen, if they knew what they were talking about, for quite a while after that—minutes, hours, even a day or two. Even when it did happen at last, on the sun, it would still be eight minutes before Earth knew anything about it. . . .

We had breakfast together, and then with no more than a glimpse of the feverish activity in the hundreds of square miles about us, and the thousands of tiny, gleaming lifeships in the State Fair grounds, Palmer Park, and wherever else there was an open space or one could conveniently be blasted clear, we were aboard. One after another the ships got the signal.

At last it was our turn. I grinned at Sammy as we came unstuck, remembering his fear that the lifeships were a cruel hoax.

Before we were clear of the atmosphere I knew the truth. Fortunately no one else did. I knew it by the way the ship handled, by the amount of fuel I was using, the amount I would still have to use, the amount I had left.

Sammy, in a way, was right. The governments of the world that was to die could have given, say, a million people a sixty per cent chance of life. It was all a question of the time and labor they had. What could be done in so long? But the multiple wasn't big enough. Not if they were to keep the multitudes quiet enough for them to have control of things at places like Detroit to run them as they had, without yelling, screaming millions fighting for life.

In the end they'd calculated to give a ridiculously small chance to a comparatively large number of people. One in 324.7, in fact. Enough to keep the world almost sane in those last few weeks.

I had sufficient fuel left, certainly, to shove us past Earth's gravitational pull, but I needed a lot more than that. Somewhere, sometime, I wanted to land. And there aren't any filling stations in space.

I thought of Father Clark and Pastor Munch and the Reverend John MacLean, still alive, still with their flock—or had their flock, the mob, found out that they had been running errands for me and torn them to pieces? They had trusted me, accepted me—but perhaps they didn't fully realize that I wasn't Simsville's instrument of God only for the three weeks of selection, but beyond that along every inch of the millions of miles of nothing between Earth and Mars.

But they could still trust me. I had promised Sammy and Leslie and all the others life, and it wasn't going to be my fault if they didn't get it.

One in a Thousand

1

Somewhere between the surface of Earth and Mars, well on the way or just about to take off, there were seven hundred thousand-odd lifeships. And believe me, the operative word was "odd." It took about a year to build a spaceship, and each and every one of these lifeships had been thrown together in eight weeks.

Problem: If two thousand skilled men can build a lifeship in a hundred days, how long will it take a thousand unskilled men to do it? Answer: 56 days. If your math's as good as mine (and mine isn't so hot) you'll get a pretty good indication of the standard of workmanship in the lifeships.

I was lying in the pilot's acceleration couch, controlling the ship with my fingertips, as far as it was being controlled at all, and hearing, seeing, and feeling the moluone fuel drain away as if it were my lifeblood. I had a simple enough choice. I could stop the blast now, and crash back on Earth; or I could let it roar out of the tanks the way it was doing, and crash somewhere else, if I ever reached anything to crash against.

When I say "in" the couch I mean just that. The couch was constructed so that I was half sitting, half lying, knees up to assist the circulation. That was a better position in which to withstand the acceleration than lying flat. I was strapped up like a mummy with imprex tape supporting my muscles. And though the couch wasn't particularly soft—it felt like solid rock—I was almost submerged in it.

But that was unimportant. What mattered was this—somehow the lifeship had to escape from Earth's gravity, and sometime it had to land on Mars. There wasn't enough fuel to do it. I could see that now, only a matter of seconds from takeoff. Ten people, lower down in the lifeship, were depending on me and on the ship for life that the ship and I weren't going to be able to give them.

I was thinking like a prairie fire, though I was practically certain there was no solution. Soon I had a little piece of an answer. My fingers moved and the blast mounted. Anyone below who had thought nothing could be worse than 6G found his mistake as the acceleration went up and up.

The ship was designed for four minutes' blasting, but if I were to save fuel there was only one way to do it. That was to get off more quickly, reach escape velocity, and stop blasting sooner, saving the fuel which would have been needed to hold the ship up during the extra time.

I refused to think about the jet linings. They were designed for four minutes' blast, presumably, and now they were being asked to take the same thrust in less time.

I nearly blacked out. I screamed and hardly heard myself.

You won't understand how I felt physically unless the same kind of thing has happened to you—when you must and do remain conscious but you're so near unconsciousness that perceptions sent along the nerve channels to your brain simply don't leave any record there. You have to notice them as they happen or you've lost them forever.

I strained my eyes at the dials in front of me, trying to make them mean that I could cut the drive. They persisted in telling the truth, which was no good to me. I saw why people sometimes strain to believe something they know is false. There are times when hopeful fantasy is much more attractive than hopeless fact.

At last I was able to cut the drive. It had been on for hours. The chronometer said it was only three minutes or so, but I knew better. It didn't stop cleanly, as it should, it eased off gently. The couch gradually rose, and I floated off, weightless.

You never quite get used to free fall, no matter how often you experience it. It's a surprise every time when up and down disappear from the environment and the normal way of getting about ceases to be beetlelike and becomes birdlike. It's amusing or frustrating, depending on how you're feeling at the time, when you want to go one way and find yourself going the other, impelled by some tiny movement of air you can't see and normally wouldn't notice at all.

The body adjusts to the new conditions more quickly than the mind. The lungs and heart and stomach, puzzled for a few minutes by the absence of gravity, soon learn their new job and do it as well as they did the old one. Clothes and hair are inconveniences, though. Practically every garment of civilization except riding breeches and bathing costumes depends to some extent on gravity to hold it in place. Whenever I moved, my jacket began to ride up about me like water wings, and my trousers gradually worked themselves in untidy folds up my legs, showing the imprex tape underneath.

I found Mars through the tungsten glass ports and began to check on the old space navigators' Irishism—whether it would be where we were when we got there. But I wasn't allowed much grace. Sammy Hoggan came in, his face grim.

"Mary Stowe's dead," he said briefly.

I couldn't understand that at first. Somebody dead—already? It interfered with my long-term calculation that we were all going to die. It jammed the works for a moment, this curious, irrelevant intimation that someone hadn't waited for the execution that appeared to be planned for us all.

"Acceleration?" I asked.

"That and her couch collapsing. It couldn't take the strain. Bill—didn't you accelerate more than you were supposed to?"

"Yes," I said.

"Then that killed her," he said bluntly. "The extra weight came on—and the couch broke. That was——"

I had heard enough about Mary, and it was too late to do anything about her. "Go away," I said.

Sammy swore. "Dammit, Bill," he said hotly, "you're responsible for all of us. You're the man in charge. Is that all you have to say? If you had to do it——"

I turned and looked coldly at him. "I'm responsible for getting this ship to Mars," I said curtly. "I'm not leaving here until I'm satisfied about that—not if the whole lot of you die. If this room had a door, I'd lock it to keep you all out. Now go and leave me alone. I'm sorry, Sammy, but I haven't time to be civil."

I went back to my calculations. I didn't notice Sammy going.

The first check was encouraging, as far as it went. There could be no precision about flying a lifeship—navigation with mass-produced instruments, and very few of them at that, was little more than an affair of pointing the ship's nose in roughly the right direction and praying.

And on this basis, it looked as if I could leave the course as it was and not waste any of my precious moluone making corrections. I wasn't too sure of our velocity—that would take days of checking by the planets—but it seemed that in about a hundred days the lifeship, in free fall, and Mars, in its orbit

66

round the sun, would have reached about the same spot.

Then, more carefully, I worked out how much fuel I'd need for a safe landing on Mars, how much I had, and tried to close the gap. Mathematically it couldn't be done. I just couldn't land safely on Mars, according to my quadruple-checked figures.

I covered sheet after sheet with laborious calculation. The best I could produce, the most favorable extrapolation, crooked, weighted mathematics though it was, was still a very slim chance indeed.

Drugged with figures, working more and more from sheer obstinacy, stubbornly trying everything I could think of to try, I came up with the conclusion that our chances of getting to Mars, when we left the soil of Earth, had been about a thousand to one against. And they weren't very much better now.

True, we were clear of Earth and on a good course for Mars. We *were* over the first hurdle. We had accomplished what, at a guess, only two or three hundred thousand of the seven hundred thousand lifeships had been able to do.

And of those two or three hundred thousand, many must have used all their fuel in tearing themselves free of Earth. Those ships were utterly helpless. Some of them would be shooting off in all directions, every moment getting farther from Mars, and utterly incapable of doing anything about it. Some of them would be pointed at the sun, or close enough to the sun to be captured by it. Some would move on and on past the planets into space . . . those ships would go on forever if they weren't captured by some star or planet.

I didn't swear or curse at anyone. I just doggedly worked out problem after problem, as if I could set everything right by my high school mathematics.

On the basis of our own experience I worked out how much fuel the lifeships really needed. Then, since they would have to be so much bigger and stronger, how many lifeships there would have been instead of seven hundred thousand. How many people they could have taken.

Allowing a very small safety factor, it came out at ninety-seven thousand. A chance of life for a million people instead of nearly eight million. Not one in three hundred of the people of Earth, but one in twenty-two hundred.

I tried to imagine the job I might have had then, the job of picking out ten people from a town of over twenty thousand. As it was, I knew hardly anything about some of the people I'd chosen from a mere three thousand or so. Sammy, Leslie, Betty, and Morgan were all last-minute choices, because someone else had had to come off the list. On the whole I was prepared to gamble on the first two, but Morgan and Betty could be my best choice or my worst for all I knew. What sort of guess could I have made if I'd been confronted with twenty thousand people and told to pick ten?

I shook my head wearily. The questions were too big for me. I had juggled too long with figures of life and death—a little life and a lot of death. They weren't anything but figures to me. Perhaps that was why I had done it—to reduce humanity's most frightful disaster to a few real figures, like four and seven and three, with a lot of incomprehensible zeroes after them.

I would come again, no doubt. But meantime I had reached a mental dead stop.

2

I gave myself a push against the wall, guided myself with my arms, and swam out into the main room of the lifeship, which Sammy had already christened, ironically, "the lounge."

Lifeships were simply moving barns. There was nothing to be seen in the so-called lounge except white paneling, steel floors, ten couches, and nine people floating about, with something on one of the couches covered by a sheet.

Little Bessie Phillips, unrepressed by tragedy, was flying about in the air, delighted by the absence of gravity. Jim

Stowe, dry-eyed, was sitting with his father, one leg curled around the frame of the couch to hold him down. Betty and Morgan were in a corner, whispering. Sammy, Leslie, Harry Phillips, and Miss Wallace formed another group, holding the edges of a couch to keep themselves still.

They couldn't help becoming suddenly silent when I came in. They knew, all of them, how I'd been supposed to take off—I'd told them myself what it would be like—and it hadn't been like that. It hadn't been as I'd said it would be. Unless something had gone wrong, unless somehow I had been forced into it, I had done something on the spur of the moment and as a result Mary Stowe had died. That was how they were all figuring it.

Maybe I had tried to be clever, they were thinking. I could see it in their faces. They were waiting for me to explain, hoping I could, pretty sure I couldn't.

I went over to Mary Stowe's couch. Nobody moved. The sheet was tied at the four corners to the frame. I untied one corner and saw what had happened.

When Mary's weight went up to half a ton or so, one of the steel supports under the couch had snapped. Then another. The couch became a switchback—and, quite naturally, Mary's back was broken.

I averted my eyes from the dead woman's face. She had not died pleasantly, and her face showed it.

"Someone help me to get the body outside," I said.

They realized that had to be done. Sammy pushed against the couch he was holding, and floated over to me. We took hold of the limp body and clawed our way to the base of the ship, to the only air lock. The eyes of the others followed us silently.

I knew I should save the dead woman's clothes, for cloth, trinkets, leather, and particularly the imprex tape which still bound her broken body might be useful in the bare, empty lifeship.

But any suggestion of stripping the body before throwing it into space would clearly heighten feeling which was al-

70

ready too high. I'd be regarded as a grave ravisher as well as a man who had made a mistake that killed Mary Stowe.

So Sammy and I left the body in the air lock, just as it was, closed the inside door, and turned the wheel that opened the outer door. There was no sound, but the air in the lock shot out into space, sweeping all that was left of Mary Stowe with it.

The body had the same velocity as the lifeship and would travel on with it. The small additional thrust imparted by the violently escaping air, however, would carry it off on a tangent. Soon the lifeship and the body of the woman who had left Earth, alive, in it would be miles apart. Then hundreds of miles. Perhaps, eventually, millions of miles.

We went back silently to the main room of the ship. Nobody seemed to have moved.

"All right," I said. "Since you're all so concerned about this thing—let's talk about it."

Harry Phillips looked up. His eyes were as kindly as ever. "Wouldn't it be better not, son?" he said gently. "You did what you thought was right. We don't doubt that."

He didn't, perhaps, but Miss Wallace didn't meet my eyes. Leslie seemed to shrink away from me, without actually moving. John Stowe, sunk in his thoughts, probably wasn't even hearing what was going on.

"Does anyone doubt," I asked, "that I had to do what I did?"

"Did you?" asked Miss Wallace bluntly, looking at me steadily. "Did you have to? Did you *really* have to?"

I cast one swift glance at her. I hadn't thought this out. But it was obvious that I couldn't explain to them all exactly what the fuel situation was. Sammy, perhaps—I'd have to share it with someone. Not anyone else, for that would mean a voyage of even greater tension, a hopeless voyage, a voyage in the course of which it would be difficult to make anyone do anything hard or unpleasant, since there would seem to be no purpose in it. So I said:

"Do you believe that I chose ten people from over three

thousand and then started off by murdering one of them?"

"No," said John Stowe, dragging himself into the present with an obvious effort. "There's no question of it being deliberate, Lieutenant Easson. But my wife"—his voice quivered—"my wife is dead. Did it have to happen? Or was it . . . unnecessary?"

I understood perfectly what he meant. It would be easier to bear if it was an accident, something that couldn't have been avoided. What was torturing him was the thought that Mary might have died because of a small, careless miscalculation. *My* miscalculation.

"You'll have to take my word for it," I said matter-of-factly, trying to freeze the raw emotion that was in the air, "that it was necessary. It did have to happen. We needed that extra acceleration. If I were doing it again, knowing someone would die, I'd still have to do it."

No one said anything, but they believed me. Stowe was nodding slowly, the dull anger and suspicion gone from the ache in his heart. The ache was still there, but it was a cleaner ache. And the others, after looking from him to me and back to him, were looking a little ashamed of themselves, ashamed of the ready assumption that because I had changed my plans I was to blame for Mary's death, ashamed that they had been so ready to think the worst.

"We always knew we had to leave the rest of Simsville behind," I pointed out. "Everyone else had to die if we were to have a chance. We accepted that, didn't we? Then let's try to think of Mary Stowe with the rest—part of Simsville we couldn't take with us."

"God damn the man who passed that couch," said Stowe through his teeth.

"He probably has," I said quietly. "Not many of the people who made the lifeships had a chance to go on one of them."

That seemed to be that. No one wanted to pursue the matter.

"Better get that imprex tape off, all of you," I said. "Roll it up carefully. We'll need it for the landing. The women can stay here and the men go down to the air lock."

Miss Wallace opened her mouth—to protest, obviously, that there was hardly any screening between the two places I'd mentioned. I waved her silent, rather impatiently.

"How much privacy do you think any of us is going to get this trip?" I demanded.

She looked around quickly, and seemed to see the force of that. She made no objection.

I had to tell someone the truth. If Pat Darrell had been along, it would have been she. As it was, Sammy was the only one I could talk to. I wasn't sure yet about Leslie. The last time she and I had been alone together, back on Earth in those last tense, terrified days, she had tried to buy her passage to Mars, and I had lunged away from her in disgust. If Pat had lived Leslie wouldn't have been there at all.

I jerked my head at Sammy, not looking at Leslie, and we pushed off and guided ourselves into the control room.

"Sammy," I said, "I've got my troubles, you know that. Mind if I share them with you?"

He grinned. "No, Bill," he said. "I may grouse and swear and be bitter about things, but that's just the way I'm made. Sure, I'll help all I can, any time. What's on your mind?"

Something in the way he said it showed me that he was remembering Pat too.

"Remember," I said, "how you once thought the lifeships were a cruel hoax? A myth designed to keep a tottering world comparatively sane while the real spaceships were granted peace to get on with their job?"

He nodded. "But you were right, Bill," he said. "I felt pretty low when I said that. It was just natural pessimism."

"It was more than that, Sammy," I said quietly.

He stared at me.

I told him. I showed him my figures—all of them.

Given only eight weeks before the sun stepped up its output enough to make Earth a 250–500° Centigrade world, the governments of the world had had no chance to transfer their people wholesale to another planet. Space travel was too young. There were too few ships. There was too little time.

No, any way they looked at it, it was a simple proportion sum. Give a few people a good chance of getting to Mars safely, or a lot of people a very slim chance.

I didn't know whether I was apologizing for them or not. I don't now. But look at it this way.

Back on Earth, at sea, a liner sinks. Nothing is left but one lifeboat and hundreds of people in the water. The lifeboat sails around and picks up people till the gunwales are nearly in the water. Then what? Others try to clamber aboard. Still more cling to the sides of the boat. What's the answer—let everyone drown, since everyone can't be saved?

Sammy was in no doubt. "The swine!" he said, his face white. "What's the use of giving people a chance that isn't a chance? Why didn't they build just as many ships as they knew could get to Mars and land there safely?"

I grinned without humor. "People will argue over that for the next thousand years," I said, "those who are left to argue about it. Me, I'd take the infinitesimal chance rather than no chance at all. But there's no use talking about it now, Sammy. It's so. What are we going to do about it?"

"What *can* we do about it?"

I let myself float comfortably on the softest cushion imaginable—air without gravity.

"A lot, in theory," I said. "The regular ships will get to Mars all right. So will some of the lifeships. There will be variations, of course—some of them will be a lot luckier than we've been, some a lot less. For some it will be a simple, straightforward trip—and if they've no fuel left after they land, what does that matter? For others it must have been a hundred per cent impossibility from the word 'go.'

"All right, there will be plenty of ships on Mars when we get there. They'll send up as many as they can to take people off lifeships that can't land safely, or help others down, or refuel them . . ."

Sammy brightened.

74

"Or," I went on, "little as we have, we certainly have enough fuel to take up some sort of orbit around Mars, and wait for someone to do something about us. There's one space suit on board. Someone could land with that, and sooner or later a ship would come up and take us off."

Sammy, looking much happier, wanted to speak, but I ignored him and went on.

"Or again," I said, "if we do nothing at all, using no fuel, we'll find one of three things happening. We may see we're going to miss Mars altogether, and if that's so we'll have to use our fuel to correct the course. We may fall into an orbit naturally, without doing a thing. Or if we see we're going to crash on Mars, we can leave the drive to the last minute and then use what we have to land as soft as we can."

Sammy began: "But that's——"

"Still not much better than a thousand-to-one chance," I told him flatly.

He stared at me incredulously.

"I'm sorry, Sammy," I said. "I know I should have kept this to myself, but I'm not big enough. Let's look at those possibilities. How many ships will there be on Mars—good ships, possible rescue ships? A few score, perhaps. And not too much fuel. How many lifeships? Hundreds of thousands. What are the few score going to be able to do for the hundreds of thousands?"

"I see," said Sammy bitterly. "Go on."

"Next, the orbit around Mars. Now it doesn't take much drive to edge a ship into an orbit around a planet. A skillful, experienced pilot could generally do it with a few seconds of blast. But, unfortunately, there are only about forty such pilots in existence, and I'm not one of them. I was a radio officer, remember. I can't do it, Sammy. I'm ready to try, but I'm no more likely to succeed than an untrained marksman is to hit a bull's-eye at five hundred yards with one shot."

"I see that too," said Sammy, his anger dropping to burning resentment against persons unknown.

"And as for decelerating safely on the fuel we have—why

we can't do it is kindergarten mathematics. Roughly, ignoring Earth and Mars altogether, we have to do as much deceleration as we did acceleration. And we have only a fraction of the fuel to do it."

"So what do we do?" demanded Sammy bleakly.

"I wish I knew. Anyway, we have weeks to think about it. Perhaps we'll be lucky. We may be one of the few lifeships that the regular ships will be able to help. Or we may take up an orbit without even trying. But . . ."

Sammy nodded gloomily. He had dropped from cheerfulness to blazing anger to black resentment to something very close to despair. "But what?" he asked.

"But we can only hope for that," I said, "not count on it." I grinned suddenly. "Cheer up, Sammy," I said. "We're not actually dead yet."

Sammy looked up sharply. "I'm not bothered about *that*," he said. "I can face the idea of dying as well as most people. I'm thinking of *Homo sapiens*. Two billion living, breathing human beings waiting on Earth to be fried. And thousands who thought they'd been saved finding now that all they'd been given was a chance to die some other way. Thousands of units of eleven people on lifeships who know now they'll never reach Mars, who know they've been sold——"

"Nobody's been sold, Sammy. The lifeships weren't a cruel hoax, as you feared. They were what it was always admitted they were—just a chance to get to another world. . . ."

But Sammy wasn't listening. I left him there and went out to make my first check of the lifeship—my first, and probably last, command.

3

We found very soon that we had far too much time on our hands. I manufactured as many jobs as I could for the ten of us to do, but there was still too little to occupy us.

There was the job of looking after the hydroponics plant on which we depended for both food and fresh air. I put Harry Phillips in charge there. He had had little or nothing to do with water-culture methods before, but he knew plants. Forced by artificial sunshine, efficient aeration of the roots, the warmth of the lifeship, and constant care, the tomatoes, potatoes, and roots grew incredibly fast in their compact

77

trays. Starvation was not going to be one of our problems. Harry's main assistant was Leslie; she or Harry was always in the plant, finding something to do. That accounted for two people.

The water purifier also had to be looked after. From it came all the water we used, and into it all the water went back. Betty and Morgan were in charge of the machine. There wasn't much for them to do, and they seemed happy together doing it. I still didn't know much about Morgan and Betty. Clearly, however, they were very much in love, and wanted no companionship but each other.

Miss Wallace was in charge of cooking. Little Bessie helped her. Bessie was a lovely, happy child. I never regretted choosing her. She was utterly unspoiled, gay but not destructive. She had consideration and sympathy rare in anyone so young. It was when I thought of Bessie that I was most determined to get to Mars safely. Bessie was going to be a wonderful woman, and not merely a very beautiful one.

Jim Stowe liked to sit in the control room and pretend to be the pilot of a spaceship. So I made that his job. He was the lookout. We didn't need one, but he liked the idea and it gave him something to do.

That left John Stowe, Sammy, and me. We helped anyone who needed help, and looked for more things for the others to do.

We kept Earth time, calling one twelve-hour period day and the next night.

On the third day two problems emerged. It was hot and stuffy, despite the fact that the hydroponics plant was dealing quite competently with the excess carbon dioxide in the atmosphere. Betty had a temperature, Morgan a streaming cold, and most of us had headaches and hot eyes.

I was in the control room explaining things to Jim when Miss Wallace came in.

"Run along, Jim," she said. "I want to talk to Lieutenant Easson."

Reluctantly Jim went. Miss Wallace surveyed me grimly, her cheeks flushed.

"Lieutenant Easson," she said formally, "something must be done about Smith and Miss Glessor. They are . . ."

I had thought at first that she was talking about their health. When I saw her expression, however, I guessed what she meant.

"They're what, Miss Wallace?" I asked.

She blushed more violently. "Openly!" she said vehemently. "With two children about!"

I didn't make her put into words what Betty and Morgan were doing.

"Well, why not, Miss Wallace?" I asked gently.

"They're not married!" she exclaimed, as if that explained everything. For her, no doubt, it did.

"Probably," I reflected, "as commander of the ship I could marry them. But we've left the old world, Miss Wallace, and I don't think things like that are going to matter for quite a while."

"Decency and moral standards always matter," she declared indignantly.

"I suppose so. But I don't think they're involved in this case. Betty and Morgan love each other, and in normal circumstances they'd be married. It didn't matter until they knew they were coming on this trip, and then it was too late. Anyway . . ."

I wanted her to see it, for if Miss Wallace saw it everyone else would. She wasn't narrow-minded—just strict and correct.

"You don't think an illegitimate child is damned, do you, Miss Wallace?" I asked.

"No, of course not. But that's not the question."

"Isn't it? We'll want as many children as possible. Frankly, there're going to be so few people in the new colony that one of the first things we'll have to ensure is that there's a big, healthy second generation——"

"Lieutenant Easson," said Miss Wallace warmly, "are you

suggesting that we should do away with marriage altogether?"

"No," I said thoughtfully, "but I don't think we can insist on it. I think what'll happen is informal marriage. People will live together and say they're married. Even if they don't—if women have children without any sort of husband in the offing—I don't think we should object."

Clearly she hadn't thought it out. She didn't refuse to entertain new ideas. It simply had not occurred to her until then that the circumstances had changed so radically that new patterns of behavior might be required, and old ones abandoned.

"Perhaps you're right," she admitted. "I'll think about it."

I talked to Betty and Morgan later. They were quiet, shy, embarrassed by the attention they had caused, but not in the least ashamed about it.

There were no doors in the ship except the air lock, and the only privacy possible was the shielding provided by the water tanks, the hydroponics plant, and other natural screens. Betty and Morgan had done their love-making as discreetly as possible, but that wasn't very privately.

"What are we to do?" asked Morgan resentfully. "Go outside into space?"

"We thought of speaking to everybody about it," said Betty, "but what could we say? It would be nonsense to ask anyone's permission . . ."

"Of course," I agreed. I told them what I had said to Miss Wallace. They brightened, glad that Authority—that was me—didn't think they had done anything wrong.

"You mean we can just say we're married," said Betty, "and we are?"

"If you like," I said. I was having a good look at them for the first time. Morgan was tall and thin, very young and immature. He was a nice-looking boy—too shy, of course, but with a friendly grin nevertheless. Betty was very small and slight, a neat little figure with corn-colored hair and small,

80

very white hands. She wore blue slacks and a yellow sweater.

At the moment Morgan's nose was red and his eyes watery; Betty was flushed and shivered frequently, her eyes too bright. They had chosen rather unromantic circumstances for their nuptials. But they insisted they felt perfectly well.

"Congratulations, anyway," I said with a grin, and went looking for Leslie. I was thinking more of Morgan's cold, Betty's temperature, and the headaches of the others than of the question of informal marriage. The marriage problem was already solved, as far as I was concerned. However, something would have to be done about the other one.

As I swam into the hydroponics plant Leslie grabbed the hem of her frock, which was floating airily somewhere in the region of her fourth rib.

"Doesn't make the slightest difference," I said. "Take it off altogether—haven't you ever worn a bathing costume?"

"Yes," she said, tucking her skirt between her legs, "but only in the appropriate circumstances."

"These *are* the appropriate circumstances." I started to explain what I meant. However, her mind was obviously on something else. I sighed, abandoned the subject for the moment, and asked what was worrying her.

She was breathing hard, obviously nervous. "I want to talk to you, Bill," she said breathlessly.

I waited. I knew at least part of why she was nervous. The last time we had been together without other people around had been an incident neither of us wanted to remember.

"I'm not sure you understand why I threw myself at your head," she said, with an effort. "It's true, I suppose, I was trying to bribe you. I wanted to live—oh, I know I was quite wrong. I've thought since about what you said. I misunderstood you completely. I——"

She wasn't getting anywhere. "Must we talk about it, Leslie?" I asked quietly. "I'll forget it ever happened, if you like."

"I don't want that. I'm trying to explain. . . . You see, I didn't know you. I wanted to live. I wasn't honest, like Pat.

What was it she said? 'I just carry on being myself without trying to buy myself a place on the ship by being someone else.' I didn't believe that at the time, but I did later. Anyway, I wasn't like that, and I knew it. I wasn't as honest as Pat, but at least I was honest with myself. I wanted to live more than anything. If you could be bribed, I was ready to bribe you."

She looked at me steadily, anxiously, trying to make me understand. "I thought it out carefully, and made sure I meant what I was doing. I had only one thing to bribe you with, and when I really thought of it honestly, it didn't seem to matter much to me. I know I was wrong—the question is, how wrong was I?"

"Not terribly wrong," I said, smiling faintly. "But I still think the least said about the whole thing the better."

"No," Leslie insisted. "Because if I meant it then, I should mean it now. Do you want me?"

I frowned. "That's mad," I said flatly.

"I don't think so," she said stubbornly. "It couldn't be a question of money, because money won't matter for quite a while now. But suppose it was money. Suppose I offered you a thousand dollars to do something, and you did it without taking the money. I'd still want to give you the thousand dollars. I'd feel you'd have to take it so——"

I burst out laughing. Leslie couldn't see the joke at first, but after a while she was laughing too. It was a ridiculous situation.

At last I said: "Leslie, I'm still turning down your bribe. I don't want you, you owe me nothing, and if you're trying to sell yourself I'm not in the market. Is that clear?"

"You're making a joke of it," she said, laughing despite herself, "and I was perfectly serious."

"Are you quite satisfied that you're not under any obligation to me?"

"Yes, if you say so."

"Right. Now that that's settled—Leslie, will you marry me?"

She stopped smiling abruptly and looked at me in amazement.

"If you feel you owe me anything," I said, "the answer's no. Or if you don't think you could possibly love me, ever. But don't say no just because you don't love me now."

"I do love you now," she whispered.

She couldn't, really; she hadn't had an opportunity. But if she thought she loved me, all the better.

We kissed, and floated in the air in each other's arms.

Later I told her what I'd had in mind when I went looking for her. She thought over what I said, and agreed. We decided to set an example right away.

I stripped to trunks and Leslie took off her dress, stockings, and shoes. "Do you think this will make enough difference?" she asked.

"No, we'll have to do other things too."

We clasped hands, pushed off from a wall, and soared into the lounge together.

"Hold everything," I said, when everyone looked up, startled, "we're not starting an interplanetary branch of the SunA. I think we should all strip, and if anyone wants to go naked altogether, so much the better."

They still stared. So I explained. "Why has everyone a headache?" I asked patiently. "Why has Betty a fever? Why has Morgan a cold?"

Sammy, Miss Wallace, and Leslie knew what I was talking about. No one else. It's amazing sometimes how obvious a thing has to become before people will see it.

"The air in here," I said, "is kept fresh enough, but the temperature is going up and up." I pointed to the white panels on the walls. "That's neutralex, and it just doesn't conduct heat at all. It's rather too efficient, in fact—combustion's going on in all of us, we're cooking food, and none of that heat's getting away. So the temperature's going up a degree at a time, and it'll keep going up until we find some way to stop it."

"Taking off our clothes won't help much," Morgan objected, and sneezed.

"True," I said, "but it's a start. The unhealthiest conditions occur when the air is warm and motionless. The skin isn't cooled and dried as it should be. In here, the hydroponics plant handles excess carbon dioxide well enough, and the water purifier mops up quite a lot of water vapor from the atmosphere. But the circulation set up by the hydroponics aeration plant is too slow to make much difference, when the temperature's so high. What we must do somehow is step up the circulation, bring down the temperature, and stop wearing clothes that we don't need any more."

Sammy threw off his sweater and pants. I caught his eye and he came over and joined Leslie and me.

"Wasn't there any provision for this?" Sammy demanded.

"Not that I know of. There's nothing we can use as a fan, but we may be able to lower the temperature."

"How?"

I swam to the wall and tapped the white paneling. "This neutralex," I said, "is simply a barrier cutting off all heat. There's no chink in it. But if we make one, we'll radiate heat at that spot."

Leslie frowned. "Space is at absolute zero, isn't it?" she objected. "Seems to me we'll lose too much heat too fast."

I shook my head. "Behind the panels is the shell of the ship. It's absorbing heat from the sun, more or less equalizing it through its whole volume by conduction, and radiating it again on the side away from the sun. Remember, there's no conduction or convection, only radiation. And balancing any heat we radiate, there's the quite considerable amount of heat radiation we're getting from the sun."

We set to work unscrewing one of the panels. As I worked, I glanced now and then at the others behind us in the lounge to see how they were reacting.

Perhaps I gave this too much importance, but as I saw it, though it might not make an enormous difference whether everybody on the ship stripped down or not, this, like the marriage question, was an index of their adaptability. They were being asked to change their behavior and ideas slightly, because circumstances had changed.

Immediately Sammy and Leslie had seen what I was getting at, they agreed—they adapted. No argument. Jim Stowe and Bessie too—Jim looked at his father, received no guidance, and threw off his shirt. Bessie didn't care in the slightest. She had no idea why we were taking off our clothes, but she obliged too, and nobody stopped her. She left only her white panties, and then, after a long, thoughtful stare at Leslie, began gravely to fashion herself a brassière out of the sash of her frock. To Bessie this was another game.

But the others whispered together and showed no sign of following our example. Well, if they didn't believe what I said, or really didn't think it mattered, I didn't mind. If, however, they were stubbornly refusing to change their ideas, it didn't augur well for a future in which they might have to do that every day for years.

4

It was on the eighth day that we found the prophecies had been right and the sun had really stepped up its output.

We had licked the temperature difficulty, more or less. We removed enough panels to set the balance right, and I tinkered with the hydroponics aeration plant to increase the circulation in the ship generally, watched by an anxious Harry Phillips. The hydroponics plant was his baby, and he didn't quite trust me with it.

Despite my assurances, Leslie and Sammy remained afraid that we would all freeze if we left the panels off—until at last, after it had been done, they saw that a nice balance had been achieved, and the temperature went neither up nor down. They also, incidentally, remained convinced for a long time that having cold spots on the walls would set up a strong air circulation and we wouldn't have to bother about that.

I explained carefully that it wasn't the expansion of heated air, or the contraction of cooled air, that set up circulation. It was a question of density—and on the lifeship, density just did not exist. Density is mass per unit volume; volume still existed, could still change, but there was no weight. Heat air on a weightless ship and it certainly expands, but it doesn't rise. It expands outward, evenly, and the compressed air around it tries to push it back evenly. There's no draft— light a match where there's no weight and no air circulation, hold it still, and it promptly goes out.

When we had achieved our temperature balance, this was clear enough to Sammy and Leslie. We had a slow circulation, without which the measures we took wouldn't have been effective at all. The cooling areas had no effect whatever on the air circulation of the ship. On the mere movement of air they had some, since as the air cooled it contracted and dragged more air in. These, however, were only eddies and had nothing to do with the movement of air round and round the ship.

On the eighth day our temperature control was functioning and checked. There had been no significant variation in more than twenty-four hours.

Sammy, Leslie, the two children, and I were still going around wearing as little as possible, and we were still the only ones who were. Morgan's cold, Betty's fever, and the general headaches had all cleared up, so perhaps the other five thought it was now unnecessary to follow our example.

Then suddenly it was hot. It couldn't have been sudden, really, but it certainly seemed so. The temperature had been adjusted so that while it wasn't cold it was always cool, certainly for those of us who were lightly clad. Leslie was in the

hydroponics plant, Sammy and I working on the water purifier, and we didn't notice the change until we found ourselves
sweating.

"The sun!" Sammy exclaimed.

We knew at once what he meant. Eight days ago had been
deadline; the sun's change might have occurred when it was
supposed to, for all we knew. It was behind us—the only way
we had of looking at it was to put on the space suit and go
out at the air lock to look back.

The change inside the lifeship, however, was so marked
that we knew almost to the minute when the sun entered its
new phase. The alloy outer skin of the ship, of course, was
absorbing extra heat; the balance we had created was gone,
and the temperature went up again.

That didn't matter much. We could handle that problem
as we had handled it before. But something else did matter.

Earth was beginning to die. Already the extra heat was
searing the world we had left. I saw Sammy's eyes cloud
and knew what he was thinking.

The polar icecaps were melting. Elsewhere, clouds of
water vapor were rising from every open body of water.
Soon lakes would bubble and gurgle; real steam would begin
to rise. The ground would crack and leaves would shrivel.
There would be earthquakes, as the wave of heat tried to
equalize itself through Earth's brittle crust.

SunAs were ecstatically offering their bodies to the new
sun, glorying in the new warmth in cold spots, throwing
away furs and heavy coats. In the warmer places the SunAs
were arching back luxuriously in the new blinding heat—and
in a few minutes screaming as it blackened their skin.

Wood houses were catching fire spontaneously, bridges
buckling, girders pushing their way through masonry and
plaster. Parched winds were rising, sweeping hissing steam
along city streets. Lamp standards buckled, water tanks
burst, glass cracked and fell in splinters.

People were running, then tripping as the sidewalks split,
screaming as their clothes began to smolder. People were

dashing into bathrooms, turning on the cold shower and being scalded by the boiling water and steam that emerged. Others, unthinking, were running for lakes and pools, unaware that the water was already well on the way to being steam. Once more the astonishing thing would be that human beings lived so long, still moving, trying to survive in a world where every tree was blazing. All over one side of the planet people who were dead, their bodies roasted, still moved and shrieked and strove for blessed coolness which no longer existed.

Now even the polar regions would be hidden under boiling clouds. Down in the depths of the sea there was still coolness, while the waters above boiled and tried to leap bodily into the atmosphere. Some deep-sea fish would still be swimming about unaware of disaster.

People on the slopes of high mountains were climbing higher and higher, and then finding abruptly that there was no escape. Even the icecaps of high mountains were turning to steam.

Hurricanes were sweeping the world, for the heat was still uneven. But they weren't cold gales—they were tearing blasts of hot air that could lift a stream bodily and never let it down.

Coalpits were burning, grassland was burning, forests were burning, whole streets in towns were ablaze. Yet there would still be freak spots in this mad world where people and animals out in the open were still alive, and water existed as water, not steam.

Now there would be volcanoes where there never had been volcanoes, the ravaged Earth adding her own contribution to the devastation. Perhaps Atlantis had risen again and was dry as a bone in a matter of minutes.

The side of Earth where it was night was having a very different, but no less frightening, experience. Tremors, sudden winds, a hot breath from somewhere, no more. Time to prepare, for obviously something was happening, something worse was going to happen; suspense, not actuality. A few minutes, even an hour or two, of reports from the other side of the world, jamming the wires and the ether—then silence. More tremors, earthquakes; the first tidal waves. And all the time the Earth was spinning, bringing millions of square miles of undevastated land into the glare, tilting seared land and boiling sea into darkness and comparative coolness—too late.

Then storms, pouring rain as water-sodden air swept around the world, cooled, and unloaded millions of tons of water on the dark land and sea. Still the world turned, giving more and more of its surface to the killing heat. Hot hurricanes were following the cool monsoons on the dark side. Already, in the night, the quarter of the Earth that remained was feeling the burning breath of the new sun. The moon was strangely bright, reflecting a stronger glare.

The part of the Earth which had been in the glare of the sun since the beginning was by this time cauterized, sterilized by heat. Nothing remained, not animals, not birds, not reptiles, not insects, not plant life. And there was no liquid for fish to live in. The bodies of the creatures which had died, if not burned, were desiccated.

But even in this part there was still life, human life. The Trogs lived—the scientific cavemen, the people who had known what was coming and prepared for it, digging deep and very special holes in the ground.

This, however, was only the start. Even when the Earth turned and there was not a square inch of ground that had not been seared by the new, more passionate sun, it was no more than a beginning. The mean temperature of the Earth, through all its mass, probably hadn't risen more than one degree yet. . . .

That was for the future—the next day, then the next. But no one would be around to see what happened in the later stages.

What brought me back to the lifeship, which was my concern, from the doomed Earth, which wasn't, was the prosaic fact that Harry Phillips was taking off his shirt.

I forced my attention back to the present, the lifeship. Earth was the past—we had known that since we left it.

It wasn't unimportant that Harry was taking off his shirt. Given the lead, Morgan Smith started to peel off his clothes too. They had thought in their various ways of the world they had left, and suddenly, perhaps for the first time, they realized they had left it and that its standards, its way of life, and the things it demanded no longer had any real meaning.

It was hot in the lifeship, stifling hot; Bill Easson was probably right after all. So they stripped, and another part of Earth died. We were no longer men and women of the third planet, the green world.

As Sammy and I unscrewed more panels on the sides farthest from the sun, there was even laughter and a suggestion of horseplay. Miss Wallace wore sensible underwear, of course. While it didn't positively deny sex, it made it look improbable. John Stowe grinned fleetingly as he looked at her—the first time he had smiled since Mary died. Morgan was flushed with embarrassment until he realized that there was no need for it, and he grinned too. Old Harry was quite unconcerned. He, at any rate, had held out for so long only because he saw no need to do as I suggested. Betty took off her slacks, but felt it necessary to explain, embarrassed, that she couldn't take off her sweater because she wasn't wearing anything underneath.

For some reason everyone thought that was very funny. Betty went redder and redder, then impulsively caught hold of her sweater to tear it off. I watched with interest that had nothing to do with sex. If Betty, the shy, nervous, self-conscious Betty, could do that, something had really happened.

But she didn't, of course.

5

There was a slightly different attitude among us after that. For one thing, Mary Stowe's death no longer seemed to be hanging over us. We all, even John Stowe, found it easier now to think of her as one of the casualties of the disaster. There had always been a lingering doubt about the truth of the scientists' predictions. We might be making fools of ourselves, and Mary might have died for nothing.

Now that was gone. We could tell from the conditions in our own little ship that all the scientists had said was justified.

92

The casual marriages of Morgan and Betty, and Leslie and me, were now accepted completely. Miss Wallace made a point of telling me that she was satisfied I was right. In fact, she said a little wistfully, if there was any question of the situation arising in her case—which, of course, there wasn't—she would gladly marry in the same conditions. Or even, she said stoutly, have children without marrying.

It was the knowledge of what had happened on Earth that did that. There is a feeling for race survival in every human being, and not only survival, but strong survival. The thought of the tiny proportion of the human race which would be left stimulated this feeling in everyone. The way people casually mentioned having children showed how their thoughts had been directed.

Morgan and Betty asked me—rather late, I suspected—when we would be safely down on Mars at latest, and whether it was all right to start children. I reassured them. Miss Wallace observed in some surprise, after long calculation, that she could still have nine or ten children. I thought that was rather an overestimate, myself. Sammy dropped a remark or two about things he was going to tell his children. Harry Phillips wondered if old people could get together on a one-child basis, so that a woman who might have another child could be partnered by a man who was past his best, and neither could be a drag on the reproduction of the younger folk. John Stowe remarked that Mary wouldn't have been able to have any more children anyway.

The attitude of the people on the lifeship still wasn't all it might be, however.

"It will be different on other lifeships," I told Leslie once. "Some crews will be finding their lieutenant turning into a little dictator."

She grinned. "I can't see you as a dictator. Your way's right, Bill."

"No, their way's right," I said. "Suppose I had to get everyone to do something in a hurry. Would they do it? Only if it suited them. They'd argue. They'd complain. Some would do it, some wouldn't."

"And I still think that's right," Leslie declared. "You must too, Bill."

"How do you work that out?"

"You picked us. If you wanted slaves you'd have picked slaves."

I had to admit that.

But I still had a point, I felt. I didn't want to give the example of the attitude I thought was right, not to Leslie.

I had married Leslie, but she didn't matter to me. She didn't figure in my calculations. That didn't mean that later, if there was a later, I wouldn't love her and cherish her and build my whole new world about her. Meantime, I was in charge of a spaceship, and having a girl was an irrelevance. If something dangerous had to be done that only Leslie could do, I wouldn't hesitate an instant before telling her to do it.

It wasn't a question of not having time for her. I had plenty of time. If it hadn't been for the fact that she still spent a lot of time in the hydroponics plant, she'd have been with me twenty-four hours of the day. What I couldn't afford to give her was attention.

We didn't get the temperature in the ship as low as it had been before, not for a long time. The hull was absorbing more heat, conducting it around, and couldn't radiate away as much from inside.

I don't know whether suggestion came into it, but apart from that possibility we proved to the hilt how much health depends on air circulation, temperature, and humidity. The water purifier's condensation unit went on strike for a day or two, and by the time we had it working again we were all like limp rags and would have lost pounds in sweat if there had been any way to measure that.

Morgan drifted all over the ship with the air current as he slept one night. He woke with a headache and fever, and for five days he had the works—cold, sore throat, headache, cough, fever. There may have been other causes, but the

94

high temperature and absence of air movement (since he went with the air) seemed to cover it.

It was Jim who suggested something I should have thought of long since. One day as he and I were in the control cabin, companionably silent, he said:

"Why can't we see any of the other ships, Lieutenant Bill?" He always called me that.

"The other lifeships, Jim?" I asked.

"Yes. There's millions of them, aren't there, all going the same way?"

"Not quite millions, Jim. Why can't we see them? Well, look. Remember all those ships at Detroit? They all took off more or less together, going from the same place to the same place. Yet I'll bet there wasn't one collision. At the end of ten seconds each ship's done about two miles. Even if you point another ship after it then and *try* to ram it, you can't do it."

I waited while he worked that out for himself. He was an intelligent kid, more intelligent than any of the adults except Sammy and Leslie. Then I went on: "Between Earth and Mars now there should be hundreds of thousands of lifeships. But the volume of space in which they may be is about—oh, say fifty million million miles. I'm sure I could make it a lot more if I tried."

I grinned at him. "So if you think of it," I said, "we're not likely to see many of the others, are we?"

"That's a pity," said Jim thoughtfully. "If there were others close, we might be able to get fuel from them."

I jerked convulsively. "How do you know we need fuel?" I demanded.

"Saw it on the meters," he said simply.

I hadn't thought there was the slightest risk of that. It wasn't a simple story that could be read from the meters at a glance. The boy must have done a lot of thinking and calculation before he could have worked out for himself what I had been careful never to hint to him.

"Have you told anyone?" I asked quickly.

"No," said Jim. "I guessed you would tell them if you wanted them to know."

I nodded. "Jim," I said, "you're going to be a useful man in the colony. When the rest of us are old, you'll be helping to run things. Just keep thinking things out as you've been doing, and you won't find much that'll beat you."

The boy flushed with pleasure. Naturally enough, I was his hero, and anything I said was worth something.

"Fuel from other ships," I mused. "I wonder."

The thought, or a germ of it, had occurred to me before and had been abandoned. Perhaps I had given it up too soon.

"I did think of that, Jim," I said. "Know why I gave up the idea?"

"Because we can't see any other ships and there may not be any in millions of miles."

"That and one or two other things. Even if there was another ship, we'd have to use fuel getting to her. At least, just now, we're not using any."

Jim nodded seriously.

"And apart from that, this other ship wouldn't have much fuel either. Certainly none to spare. What would we do, fight for what it had? Take the people in the other ship aboard? If lifeships could hold twenty, there would be twenty in them. Anyway, how would we transship them? Each ship carries only one space suit . . ."

But as I went on detailing the objections it seemed more and more that we should at least look into the matter.

"Jim," I said, "go and get Sammy and Leslie."

He came erect excitedly. "Can I come back with them?" he asked.

"Sure—you're the assistant pilot, aren't you?" I stopped him as he was about to dive through the doorway. "Don't let anyone know there's anything going on," I warned. "Be casual."

He went more slowly.

Leslie and Sammy were in the control room with us in two minutes.

I hadn't told Leslie about the fuel situation, but she didn't turn a hair when I did tell her.

"I guessed it," she said.

"I wonder if anyone else has?" I said. "Here's four of us who know about it. That only leaves six who don't. Do you think I'm right to try to keep it secret?"

"As long as you can," said Sammy. "But when you can't, the others may as well know the truth. I don't think things would be as bad as you believe, Bill. They're good people. They wouldn't go to pieces."

We discussed Jim's suggestion. I asked him to state it himself, and it was obvious how proud he was to be included in our council.

"That's all very well," said Sammy. "But since we can't see any other ships . . . ?"

"We haven't tried," I said. "We only have an angle of vision of about 150° here. The first step is for me to go out at the air lock in the space suit and scan space behind us. There may be a ship within a hundred yards."

"Not you," said Sammy definitely. "Me. There may not be much risk, but if anything should happen to the man who goes out, he'd better not be the one man who can operate this ship."

I nodded. "No time like the present," I said. "Let's go now."

The others didn't pay any particular attention to us as we went through the lounge. Sammy and I or Leslie and I were always working on something. There was no indication that there might be anything special about this occasion.

We started to put the space suit on Sammy. The hydroponics plant was between us and the other six; they might see us, but we couldn't help that.

"You'd be more comfortable with your clothes on for this," I said. "But you needn't stay out long."

He had the whole suit on except the helmet when we discovered something that had been missed when we checked the suit.

The helmet wouldn't fit on the suit—not with Sammy's head in it. It was flawed, like the acceleration couch that had broken, like hundreds of other things, probably, in thousands of other lifeships. The outside was perfectly machined, the heavy steel base and the tungsten glass face plate were perfect. Everything was perfect, except that inside the dome was a jagged, irregular lump of metal that rested on the top of Sammy's head and wouldn't let the base of the helmet meet the ring on the suit. There was a gap of four and a half inches all the way.

Sammy, who had been quite even-tempered for a long time, forgot Leslie and Jim and swore long and bitterly.

We should have tried the helmet on our heads before, of course, instead of deciding it was all right because it looked all right. But there wasn't any more we could have done about it than we could do about it now.

I tried it on my head. The space between base and ring was even bigger.

We had hopes of Leslie—the gap was smaller and it seemed for a moment that if we padded her shoulders so that all the free space was at the top of the suit we could force the ring on it high enough to meet the base of the helmet. The arms were the trouble. Some suits have mechanical arms operated from inside the suit, but not this one. True, we could get the suit on Leslie with her arms pinned at her sides. Then, however, she would be completely helpless, unable to operate even the air lock, and certainly not the propulsion unit. If she went out like that she would fall into space and be lost.

"I don't know," I said, "whether to laugh or cry."

"I do," said Sammy gloomily. "You three cry, and I'll laugh."

Sammy had the misfortune to be a tragedian with all the gestures and expressions of a comedian. Leslie and I grinned, and Jim gave a surprisingly adult chuckle. Both Jim and Bessie always found Sammy a great joke.

I felt better for a moment, but only a moment. I hadn't taken the matter as seriously as Sammy at first. I was something of a handy man; the thought of a little metalwork didn't disturb me in the slightest. However, as I ran over in my mind everything we had in the empty, naked lifeship, my face changed, and Leslie noticed it.

"Isn't there *anything* we can do?" she asked.

With even a hammer and chisel we might have chipped the flaw away in time. We could improvise a hammer, but what could we use as a chisel?

"You don't need to do anything," said Jim earnestly. "The suit will go on me. I'm sure of it."

I looked at him thoughtfully. "That's probably true, Jim," I said slowly. "But you don't mind if we try a few other things first?"

"Oh, I don't mind," Jim said confidently. "But it'll be me all right. You'll see."

Sammy and I scouted around the whole lifeship, looking at everything, picking it up and trying it. Practically all the loose metal objects were thin aluminum.

We abandoned all idea of secrecy. We showed the helmet to the others and asked for ideas. A host of impracticable suggestions were immediately forthcoming. We laughed at some of them—it was all great fun, a sort of parlor game in which we all joined, not Hunt the Slipper but Who Can Wear the Space Suit? We tried it on everybody, with much hilarity.

With Betty we nearly made it. The helmet and its fitting actually met. However, that was the limit—tightening it down could only drive the metal in the dome through the top of her head. We thought of an airtight collar above the ring, but there was no way to make one. We chipped at the metal with all the substitutes for a hammer and chisel we could find, and managed to scratch it, no more.

Someone suggested acid, and by pooling our knowledge we found that hydrochloric acid was hydrogen and chlorine, that you could make it with salt and sulphuric acid, and that you could make sulphuric acid with sulphur trioxide. Which was very interesting but didn't help, since none of us really knew how to do it, and we couldn't risk tampering with the hydroponics chemicals and the water purifier to get the stuff.

"It looks," I said at last, after we had tried everything we could think of, "as if you're right, Jim. It's got to be you or little Bessie."

"What's that?" asked Stowe sharply.

And it wasn't a joke any more. As Sammy had said, though there wasn't much danger in going outside a ship in a space suit, there was always a risk. A score of things that we couldn't check any other way might turn out to be wrong with the suit. Jim might be blown out with the air. The lock might stick. The little things that might happen would be nothing to a spaceman, but they might well be fatal to a thirteen-year-old boy.

Theoretically I could give any orders I liked, and they had to be obeyed. But I couldn't let Jim go out unless his father agreed. After all, Stowe had already lost Mary.

I told them we needed fuel. Though I didn't say how serious it was, I made it clear our chances would be much better if we could get some from somewhere. And we had just demonstrated that any space-suit work that had to be done, Jim Stowe would have to do.

"No!" exclaimed John Stowe, as I expected. "Mary's dead —now you want to risk Jim!"

I waited. I saw Stowe struggling with himself. "I'd go," said Stowe at last. "But not Jim—please, not Jim."

"You can't," I told him. "If it were possible, we'd do it ourselves. Only Jim can do it—or Bessie. Do you want it to be Bessie?"

It was Jim himself who swayed the balance in the end. "Please, Dad," he begged. "Can't you see I've got to do it? But I won't if you say no."

I wasn't quite honest about all this. I couldn't afford to be. There was small risk in sending Jim out to have a look back the way we had come. But if he did happen to see another ship, and if we decided to contact it, Jim would have to do it. And that would be very dangerous indeed.

I knew that if Stowe said yes once he'd have to say it twice. This wasn't just his permission for Jim to do a simple, fairly safe job. It was his agreement for Jim to do any space-suit job that was needed, no matter how dangerous.

He didn't know that. He said, "Yes." And we began to get Jim ready.

There was no trouble. Jim was out a long time, but he battered on the hull occasionally, as I'd told him to do, to let us know that all was well and he was just taking his time. I was as impatient as Stowe, asking myself what Jim could be doing all this time, and wondering, unworthily, whether he wasn't just playing, pretending to be a spaceman doing a dangerous repair job on a damaged ship.

But then I remembered how careful Jim was and realized that he wouldn't come in until he felt absolutely responsible for what he had to say, and could tell us, not "I think," but "I know."

I said this to Stowe when he spoke anxiously. He seemed comforted.

"You like Jim, don't you?" he said.

"I'd rather risk Leslie than him," I told him. Leslie heard that. She smiled at me approvingly, but I saw she didn't be-lieve it. Leslie wasn't an anxious, jealous wife. She wasn't unsure of herself, or of me. I might not love her as some men had loved some women, but there were already strong ties of affection between us, and she knew it.

What I said was true, nevertheless. I'd rather risk Leslie than Jim. Leslie would play her part in the new colony, if we reached it, and play it well. She would never be, how-ever, the asset Jim might be.

Jim came in at last. His teeth were chattering as we helped him out of the suit—the big suit, apparently, absorbed less heat from the sun and radiated more than the hull of the ship.

"There's a lifeship not more than a few miles behind us," said Jim clearly. "I waited till I was sure it was moving the same way and at the same speed as us. I couldn't see anything else anywhere that could be a ship."

I almost refused to believe him. This had just been something to try, and when it duly failed we'd be no worse off.

"You're sure?" I asked foolishly—obviously he was sure. The others began to chatter excitedly, glad to know we weren't as alone in space as we'd thought. I grinned at Sammy. "What has the voice of doom to say now?" I asked.

"Nothing. It's his day off," said Sammy apologetically.

"The sun," Jim told us, puzzled, "looks very small and far away. I thought it would be big and bright, Lieutenant Bill. But it's not."

6

There was really something to think about now. Did we want to contact the other ship? How was it to be done? Should we try to communicate with it first?

If we were going all out for contact with other lifeships, I could try to turn ours so that it was facing back to Earth but flying on in the same course. Then we could spend hours in the safety of the control room scanning space for other ships. We might easily find some. Space is clear—vision without the impedance of atmosphere is so sharp and exact that we might see the pinpoint of reflected light that meant a lifeship hundreds of miles away.

That course of action was almost out of the question, however. The regular ships have gyros and jets that can turn a ship without interfering with its line of flight, but not the lifeships. Anyway, sooner or later I'd probably have to turn it back.

"Seriously," said Sammy, when he and I were alone, "has Jim much chance of getting to that other ship and back in the space suit?"

"Oh yes," I said. "That's easy enough. Depends on who's in the suit, of course. If it had been Betty, say, I don't think I'd have let her try it. But though Jim's young, he's got guts and brains. That's not the problem."

"Then what is?"

"The other ship. There're people on it, alive or dead. Another lieutenant. People who want to get to Mars. Suppose they have no fuel left at all. Suppose their hydroponics plant isn't working, or their water purifier. Or suppose they have illness aboard. Suppose——"

"Don't suppose any more," said Sammy bitterly. "I see. It's like everything else since this impossible trip began. Nothing right, nothing as it should be. Nothing but difficulty, trouble, things going wrong——"

"Hold on, Sammy," I said, laughing. "Count ten, and if that's not enough, count a hundred. We've been very lucky indeed. We had a perfect takeoff, so perfect that I didn't have to do any course correction—it was never wrong. No trouble with the hydroponics plant, nothing we couldn't put right on the water purifier, no leaks, no failures, no illness to speak of, no fights, no quarrels, nothing we couldn't solve except this thing that we may be solving now. Then even when the space suit was wrong for the people who would have used it, we had an excellent spaceman to take over. And whenever we think of contacting another ship, we look out the back door, and there she is!"

"Maybe," said Sammy morosely, "but you didn't mention Mary Stowe dying and . . ."

"And what?"

"Oh hell," said Sammy with a reluctant grin. "Get on with it."

We discussed the problems painstakingly. Sammy, his pessimism gone for the moment, agreed that despite everything against it we had to contact the other ship.

Leslie agreed too, when she came into it. "But have you worked out just what you're asking of Jim, Bill?" she asked gravely. "He's got to deal with a whole lifeship complement alone—speak for us, decide for us. I mean, he'll be there, and we won't. He'll have no one to ask, no one to help him. And if for any reason at all he doesn't come back, we can't do a thing. We haven't another suit. He could get back to the air lock and suffocate there, for all we could do to help him."

Sammy looked a little ashamed of himself. That was the crux of the matter, not the objections he had made.

"Let's put it to Jim," I said.

"No," Leslie objected. "We know what he'll say. He'll do it. But he's only a child, Bill. We have to be careful what we ask him to do. Little Bessie would walk trustingly out of the air lock without a space suit at all if you asked her, but the fact that she did it willingly wouldn't relieve you of any responsibility."

"I know," I said. "But from the standpoint of pure reason there's only one answer. If Jim doesn't go, we haven't much chance. If he does, the chances of all of us, including him, may go up a lot. We've burned our boats by telling the others we need fuel. As you say, Leslie, we know how Jim himself will feel about it. Let's call Stowe into this, shall we?"

Poor Stowe was in a terrible state. We couldn't conceal from him any of the dangers. He tried to speak, but didn't know what to say. As I'd known at the time, I'd hamstrung him when I got him to say yes before.

"I wish there hadn't been a ship near," he muttered at last, not looking at us. "Then we'd have had to make the best of it. But now . . ."

I knew he felt it too. We had gone too far in this matter to go back. After all, the other ship was there. We could almost feel it behind us, following us; we couldn't forget it or pretend it wasn't there.

"Look on the other side," I urged, wishing Leslie wasn't watching me, knowing I was raising hopes which might never be realized. "Suppose Jim finds fuel. If he does, if there's enough—our worries are over. Ships don't crack up in space, you know that. All they ever have to worry about is taking off and landing. More fuel, and we're safe. Jim too."

"If he was your son," said Stowe with an effort, "would you let him go?"

"Yes," I said without hesitation.

"I believe you. We need this fuel?"

Oh, let it go, I thought. "We have to have it," I told him.

Stowe squared his shoulders. "Then there's nothing more to say, is there?" he said, trying to smile.

We packed Jim up in warm clothes, checked every part of his suit, the tiny propulsion unit, and the air tanks. I made sure that he knew what to do in every emergency I could think of, told him all about the moluone fuel we needed— what it looked like, how we'd handle it, how much we needed; I impressed on him again and again that he was on his own and that anything he tried he had to manage himself, without help from us.

I stopped at last when I saw that, though he was excited, he had a pretty good idea of what he was doing, and any further instructions would only be an encumbrance to him.

I knew from the way Stowe said good-by to him that he was certain Jim would never come back. He was fighting the idea for all he was worth, but it had taken a firm hold on him.

I'd never believed there could be so much tension among us as there was when he was gone. Normally our life was easy, lazy. Some of us who didn't want to get out of condition or fat—Sammy, Leslie, Harry, Miss Wallace, and I—exercised as much as we could in the absence of weight. But for the most part we relaxed and slept or dreamed or thought or merely drifted about. All of us had found hours passing in the apparent space of minutes. Tension didn't exist as a normal part of existence.

But whether we were concerned about Jim himself, about what he was trying to do, what he might find, or what might happen to him, the result was some surprising things.

When Bessie pulled at Leslie to tell her something, Leslie snapped: "Don't bother me just now." Bessie wasn't hurt—she merely stared at Leslie in wonder. Leslie made a gesture as if to caress the child and tell her it was all right. Then she remembered Jim and frowned anxiously again.

Sammy, who rarely clowned, was swimming about grotesquely in the air. He pulled faces at Bessie, and she forgot the strange impatience of Leslie and laughed delightedly.

"I wish I could have gone," said Betty.

"What could you have done, poppet?" asked Morgan teasingly. "It's not a job for a pretty little baby like you."

"It's a job for anyone who can do it," said Betty warmly. "That's why Jim's gone."

"Might have asked him to go on back to Earth while he was at it, and see what it's like there now," said John Stowe, and laughed as if he had made a very good joke and had only just fully appreciated it.

Sammy swirled around the whole group, his face screwed into a fiendish mask, and Bessie screamed with pleasure.

"I didn't want one of those hard, capable girls who do things like men, honey," said Morgan affectionately.

"You wanted someone like me, someone who's no use for anything?" asked Betty with a tinge of resentment.

"Oh, I wouldn't say you're no use for *anything*," said Morgan meaningly.

"That's all you care about me."

"For heaven's sake! I only said——"

"I heard what you only said. And I know what you only meant. I'm just someone to sleep with."

"Oh, go chase yourself."

"Hold it, kids," I said wearily.

"I'm not as useless as you think," Betty said.

"Well, it seems to me you're being pretty useless at the moment, darling. When you go on about something I never said you're about as useful as a sick headache."

"It's nice to know what you really think of me, anyway. It's nice to get at the truth. I should be glad I'm useful for something, I suppose."

"Even at that," said Morgan, "you're not so damned hot."

I don't know who hit whom first. I wasn't watching them. We stared for a moment—they were so close, so quiet that we couldn't imagine them fighting, even after the build-up they'd been giving themselves. But they were certainly fighting. Morgan slapped Betty's face with savage force that sent her flying across the lounge and him back against the opposite wall. Betty, instead of bursting into tears as we immediately expected, threw herself at him and struck at his face ineffectually. Morgan hooked his foot in the frame of one of the couches and raised his arm high, a maniacal expression on his face. I dived from the wall and butted him in the midriff with my head as his arm came down. He spun crazily in the air, nursing his ankle, and I bounced back from him.

Betty burst into tears then. There was an immediate reconciliation, and no one said much about the incident.

But I looked on Morgan with some suspicion after that. Back on Earth, if a man tried to interfere with a girl and her escort killed him with a bottle he happened to be holding in his hand, he might get off with a light sentence. But if he waited to light a cigarette, then pulled out a gun and shot the other man, it would be a death sentence.

It seemed to me there was that essential difference in what Morgan had done. If he had thrown himself at Betty and battered her, I could forget it. There was something unpleasant, however, about the way he had anchored his foot so that he could smite the girl with all the power of his body unhampered by weight. I didn't know where he was going to hit her, but he could have killed her with a blow like that. The presence of mind he had shown in his act made it startlingly sadistic.

108

And then Leslie started looking for a fight too. "You shouldn't have let Jim go," she snapped at me. "A child like that . . ."

So I was the only one responsible. I had thought we all agreed that Jim had to go. "Can it, Leslie," I said as pleasantly as I could. "Suppose—just suppose—he's finding us more fuel? Try thinking of that, will you?"

"Fuel, fuel—you've got fuel on the brain."

"So I have. People need it, you know, to fly spaceships. Even me. And that's what I'm trying to do at the moment."

"The man with one idea. I believe you'd sell me, too, for this precious fuel of yours."

"Sure I would. Who are you that you shouldn't be sold?"

"For the love of God!" Stowe shouted, his nerves worn raw.

"Sorry, John," said Leslie quickly. "Sorry, Bill. Let's all shut up, shall we, before we start wringing each other's necks."

"Amen," said Sammy, and looped the loop. We fell into an uneasy silence.

No, it wasn't pleasant waiting. I knew Jim would be gone a long time anyway—the most economical way to use his little propulsion unit was merely to put himself in a slow drift toward the other ship and wait patiently till he got there. But that didn't prevent us from worrying, long before he could have reached the ship.

Morgan and Betty went out of the lounge together. I looked after them, frowning—if they fought again, and no one was around to stop him, Morgan in his wild rage might do something we should all regret. It was unlikely, however, that their reconciliation could last such a short time.

The first moment when Jim might reasonably have returned came and went. I wished there was something I could have set everyone to do. I thought of Morgan and Betty, and wished I could go away with Leslie and pass the time in her arms. I looked at them, smooth and cool, and ached for her. Leslie wanted it too, I saw. But any moment now Jim should be back. He was approaching the limit of his air supply.

John Stowe said as much, suddenly admitting his anxiety.

"You know Jim," I said reassuringly. "He'll wait as long as he can, making sure the job's done."

"How long are we going to wait, before we admit he isn't coming back?"

I answered calmly, "We needn't start thinking along those lines for quite a while yet. He doesn't need as much air as an adult, and for the most part he won't be active."

"But——"

"Remember when he was out before? Remember how he took his time, making sure?"

"I'm going to the air lock," said Stowe abruptly.

"Oh, all right. I'll come with you."

I had told everybody to stay away from the air lock because I was afraid someone would do something wild like trying to open it to see if Jim was coming. Some people can never comprehend a vacuum—they know they can't stick their heads out in space because they've been told, but they never see why. They have some vague idea that if they hold their breath it will be quite safe.

No one needed to be at the air lock, anyway, because if Jim could reach it he could certainly operate the doors. But inevitably, very soon after Stowe and I went there, we were all crowded in the cramped spaces at the stern of the ship. It was cold there. That was where the air circulation was strongest, and where most of the cooling of the air was done. I realized that it had been quite cool for days. The hull must be absorbing less heat from the sun, allowing more to radiate away, and gradually the temperature was dropping again.

Morgan and Betty were with us again. Morgan was silent and withdrawn. Betty was shivering. There was something pathetic about Betty; it was partly her youth, partly her helplessness, partly her slightness. She had made herself a bra long since, not to be different from the others by going on wearing her sweater. Clad as she was, her small body was

110

thin and fragile. Her ribs showed plainly, her legs were too thin, and her shoulder blades stood out sharply in her back. She wasn't unattractive, but beside Leslie, who was as slender as a beautiful girl could be and still be called beautiful without reservations, Betty was thin and bony.

I didn't see how Morgan could possibly hit her. It was like hitting little Bessie. Leslie was different. There could be physical rivalry with a girl like Leslie.

God, it was time Jim was back.

I knew that if I had to go through the whole thing again I wouldn't let Jim go. I searched desperately for something to say, anything that wasn't about Jim.

"I think we could put a couple of the panels back, Sammy," I said. "There and there. The radiation isn't so——"

The wheel that closed the outer door began to turn. Stowe jumped to spin it. I grabbed his arm.

"Let Jim do it himself," I said thankfully. "He may have a leg in the doorway or something."

When we saw that the outer door was tight shut, however, I threw back the inner lock. Air whistled past us and filled the empty lock.

There's not much that can change faster than human beings' moods. It took us only about half a second to transfer our concern from Jim back to the fuel question. We saw through the face plate that he was all right; instantly all of us except Stowe forgot our anxiety and began to babble excitedly about what he might have found, while Sammy and I started to unscrew the nuts that secured his helmet.

"He's back—it must be all right," said Betty, with baffling logic.

"I knew he'd do it," said Stowe, wildly distorting the truth in his relief.

"Maybe we'll have our nineteen children after all," Leslie told me, grinning.

"But if there *is* fuel, how are we going to get it here?" asked Harry, seeing that problem for the first time.

"Easy," I said. "It doesn't weigh anything, and in space

it hangs together by surface tension. All we have to do is——"

"Get on with your job, Easson," grunted Sammy, "and don't count your chickens before you've got any eggs."

We got the helmet off and looked expectantly at Jim.

"I'm sorry, Lieutenant Bill," he said. "There's nothing in that ship—no air, no fuel, no people, no anything. It's empty!"

We stared at him, the excitement and expectancy slowly disappearing from our faces. It had always been a wild hope, but we had let ourselves believe in it. When I saw Jim back, I too had allowed myself to think, for no reason at all, that he must have been successful.

I forced myself to say calmly: "Oh well, we'll have to do the best we can." Jim was almost in tears, as if it was his fault— no wonder, with everyone looking at him in silence, all hope and pleasure in his return wiped off their faces and nothing left but blankness and despair. Somehow we had worked out, as Betty had, that if only Jim came back safely there would be nothing to worry about. "Cheer up, Jim. You did very well. You couldn't find fuel if there wasn't any there."

Betty, more from strain than anything else, burst into tears and threw herself into Morgan's arms.

"I always saw myself as a tragic hero," said Sammy, not very helpfully. But he made amends by ruffling Jim's hair and telling him: "Bill's right, Second Lieutenant. It's not your fault the tanks were empty, not fuel."

Jim, whose sense of humor wasn't as adult as most other things about him, chuckled involuntarily. And if we still felt despair at Jim's report, at least we didn't force it on everyone else. We came to life again, smiled and talked and pretended the whole incident was merely a welcome break in the monotony of our existence.

But it was our lowest point on the trip so far, worse than when Mary died, worse than when we knew Earth was burning. You never know how black things can look until your hopes have been raised and then dashed again.

7

I left Jim with his father and the others for a few minutes, to
let them all realize that he was safe and had done his job well,
even if he hadn't been successful. Then I set Stowe, Harry,
and Morgan on the job of refitting two of the neutralex panels
and took Jim, Leslie, and Sammy into the control room.

Jim couldn't understand what had happened to the other
ship, and neither could I. He had noticed long before he
came to it that there were no lights in the control room, but
that wasn't surprising. When we were all in the lounge there
were no lights in our control room either.

The first shock was when he found the outer air-lock doors open. He closed them and opened the inner door. There was no rush of air. Everything was black. He had to shine his torch to find the lights. They went on at once.

The ship was almost as empty as if there had never been people in it. Not quite; he found a handkerchief and a girl's stocking. The log hadn't been opened—there wasn't a line in it.

The plants in the trays were dead; the water purifier seemed to be working. Nothing was broken except one of the meters in the control room. The fuel register was at zero. There was no space suit on the ship.

"I wondered," said the boy tentatively, "if they hadn't already transferred to another ship. With two suits, theirs and the one in the other ship, they might have ferried people across one at a time . . . ?"

"It's the only reasonable explanation, Jim," I said, "but I'd like a better one."

Where was the other ship? Why had they left the ship that was on a perfect course for Mars, when they could have transferred fuel from the other?

"How about supplies?" I asked.

"They hadn't been touched," said Jim. "Vitamin tablets, concentrates, synthetic protein . . . I left them, because we have enough, haven't we?"

"Quite right, Jim." But that made it even more incomprehensible. If they had transferred to another lifeship, they would need their own supplies.

"Could they have been picked up by a regular ship?" Leslie asked.

"It's possible. That would explain a lot. But the regular ships would be packed with all the people they could carry."

We had to leave it at that. Every one of those seven hundred thousand ships had a story, some merry, some tragic. And we had hit on one of the mysteries. What seemed to me most likely, after considering the possibilities, was that one of the regular spaceships had had to take off in a hurry, half empty. Perhaps, in the center of a riot after the lifeships had gone and the people of the world were one crazed mob left behind to die, a spaceship had had to blast off in a hurry or not at all. Naturally enough, if that was so, it would match velocities with lifeship after lifeship, taking off people who otherwise had a much smaller chance of reaching Mars safely.

And if so, we had been just one ship too late. With the one Jim had examined the regular ship had reached its limit and blasted on toward Mars. It would probably be there now, safe. It's difficult to imagine the difference between the regular ships and the lifeships if you don't know it. The regular ships could take three hours, if they liked, to reach a thousand miles up from Earth; they could maneuver in space better than an airplane in an atmosphere; they even, some of them, had artificial gravity of one sort or another— magnetic or centrifugal, mostly—so that people could go from Earth to Mars as comfortably as from New York to London. Only it had never been necessary to transport more than a few hundred people a year between the planets.

Sammy, of course, realized that this was what had probably happened and that we had just missed rescue. "Our usual luck," he said morosely.

"I checked that all the fuel was really gone," said Jim. "I climbed into the firing chambers. The blast had never been cut at all. It was just left till all the fuel was gone."

"Well done, Jim," I said. "I can't think of any more you could have done."

"There *was* something else," he said hesitantly, not wishing to appear to be boasting. "I was a long time in space both ways, and I spent most of the time looking for other ships. The sky is full of pinpricks of light, and it's difficult to pick out anything for sure. But I saw that both our ship and the other lifeship had a bluish tinge. I looked for any other spots of light with that blue tinge about them . . . there weren't any I could be really sure about."

He looked at Sammy a little nervously, perhaps expecting him to explode in bitter fulminations against somebody or

Fate. He gulped, aware of his responsibility in positively denying something that none of us could check, or affirming something that might be wrong.

"There was one little speck that might be a lifeship," he said at last. "I could hardly be sure it was there. Away out toward Saturn."

"Could you get to it, Jim?" I asked.

"I might. But . . . I don't think I could get back. If this ship behind us is six miles away—and I think it's probably quite a lot more than that—the other ship must be at least a hundred miles away." He added, apologetically again: "I'm not really sure it's there at all."

Then contacting other lifeships was out of the question. I could use our fuel to get nearer the second ship Jim mentioned, but it was too big a risk, and not worth it.

"We may as well forget other lifeships," I said. "It was a chance, that's all. Never mind, Jim. It was worth it anyway."

The days slipped past. Sammy really had very little to complain about. I could think of a lot of unpleasant things that might have happened to us that didn't, and a lot of respects in which we were fortunate.

The course was one thing. I wasn't responsible for that. The men at Detroit who had set up the ship and trimmed the jets had done a magnificent job. Every new calculation I made showed more clearly that we were going to hit Mars fairly and squarely, without a single blast for course correction. That isn't precisely what you'd expect. The wildest optimist would hesitate about suggesting that you could set up a ship on the surface of Earth so accurately that mere blasting free into space would send it directly to Mars—or where Mars would be when it got there.

If we did get through, if we did land safely, the real credit would go to the men who had trimmed the ship. Even if we didn't, it was already clear that they had done all they could for us. And if we didn't get through, who would? Certainly not the ships that had had to correct their course just clear of Earth's gravitational pull, again on the way, and a third time as they neared Mars.

I haven't mentioned the things that went off pretty much as expected. The air inevitably became a little stale; we couldn't wash it out thoroughly. There were grouses about that. Food from a hydroponics plant is all very well, but there was a sameness about it that made some of us want to scream. Potatoes, water, synthetic protein, vitamin tablets, tomatoes, sugar, lemon juice, carotene, and all the rest of it —eating on the lifeship wasn't interesting or enjoyable, and we all felt permanently unsatisfied and dreamed of steaks and fried chicken. But all the same, food was never a problem. There were no signs of malnutrition. All the hydroponics plant and our meager supplies were meant to do was keep us alive and reasonably healthy, and they did that perfectly efficiently.

Some of us missed tobacco. I didn't—I had been a smoker, but I saw so clearly before the trip started that living was more important than smoking that I hardly thought of it after that. Not smoking was part of life on the lifeship, like the weightlessness.

Exercise wasn't missed as much as we'd have thought. You don't need as much exercise when you can relax utterly, and we all learned that. We became capable of floating so limply in the air that a mere hint of a draft would roll us over, bend our limbs, wag our heads. Relaxation like that just isn't possible when gravity is present.

For the exercise that was necessary we instituted a sort of sports day that was held regularly. The purpose wasn't competition, it was primarily to use muscles that otherwise wouldn't be used at all. The sports became more complicated every time as we adapted ourselves more and more to the conditions.

There was Four-five-bump, for example. You had to start out from one wall, touching five walls with left hand, right hand, left foot, right foot, and head, and bumping on the last with what Harry Phillips called your Sunday face. The whole thing was timed, and the winner was the person who could do it most quickly. The usual winner was Bessie, presumably because she was the most adaptable among us. None of the rest of us could get the trick of doing the whole thing as a concerted action the way she did.

There was the arm race, a race across the lounge without a push-off, using only the arms to propel you through the air. Again strength didn't count. It was Miss Wallace who made the best use of arms and air resistance, pulling herself rapidly along with slow, strong strokes.

There was wrestling, in which a fall was a touch against any wall. Sammy and I would wrestle, then Leslie and Miss Wallace, Betty and Jim, and so on until we all ganged up on Bessie, to her delight.

I think generally we must have been one of the happiest lifeship crews among the seven hundred thousand. And it made me proud, for I felt I had chosen well. Only after Morgan Smith's name was there any sort of question mark.

As we were nearing Mars Stowe married Miss Wallace. The rest of us were faintly surprised, but realized when we thought about it that it was a good thing. Stowe was a little defiant, in case anyone suspected he had forgotten Mary, or that she hadn't meant much to him. But I think we all knew better. After all, it was a long time since Mary died.

Miss Wallace was really rather young for Stowe, but she didn't look it. We had always called her Miss Wallace; now, when she became Mrs. Stowe, we began to call her Caroline. It was only then that we learned her first name.

Her marriage was no more formal than those of Betty and Morgan, Leslie and me. But one automatically made the change and thought of her as Mrs. Stowe. That wasn't the case with the rest of us. Betty was just Betty, and I had never thought of Leslie as Mrs. Easson. If this casual marriage became common, I could see the custom of the woman taking the man's name dying out altogether. Miss Wallace wanted to be Mrs. Stowe, but Betty preferred to remain Betty

Glessor, and Leslie, when she once signed her name in the log, signed it "Leslie Darby."

"Now I'm left all alone," said Sammy. "Will you marry me, Bessie?"

"Yes," said the child instantly, "if you'll stop looking so black."

8

Mars was big in the forward window now. The first of the three big questions was already settled.

The three questions were: Would the ship miss Mars? Would it take up an orbit around it? Would it crash plumb into it? I wanted them settled, if possible, before I did anything at all.

It was clear that the ship wasn't going to miss Mars. I had been spending hours in the control room looking at it and wishing I was a better pilot.

Spaceships at best—I mean the regular spaceships—can't

afford extra people on board. The crew is always at a minimum. That means that in emergencies everyone must be able to do someone else's job. As well as being a radio officer I had been fourth pilot. I had taken up and landed ships—big ships, ships they trusted me not to smash. But always I had an experienced pilot at my side, ready to take over. Always I'd had painstaking, quadruple-checked calculations on which I could and did trust the ship and my life and everybody else's life. Always, most important of all, I'd had plenty of fuel in reserve, so that if I was at all doubtful I could blast clear and try again.

In those circumstances I wasn't a bad pilot. I had been passed without hesitation—indeed, with the utmost confidence—as a lifeship pilot, and the question of further training and practice hadn't arisen. After all, seven hundred thousand pilots had to be found. If any had to be trained specially for the job, it certainly wasn't the few men who had actually flown a regular ship, ever.

But I knew that Mart Browne or Colin Mitchell, say, two of the pilots I'd worked with, would merely glance at the controls of the lifeship and at Mars and know exactly what they could do and what they couldn't. By feel they could put the ship in an orbit, with the fuel I had, if that seemed the best thing to do. And either of them, I felt, could have a healthy stab at the job of setting the ship down—again, on the fuel I had.

Some lifeships would be lucky that way. They would have trained, experienced pilots, and men like that, given half a chance, would do the almost impossible. Others, perhaps, would be lucky in having in charge someone who didn't know the difficulties, someone who would come through without having any idea of the various disasters he'd just missed.

I had the little learning that was a dangerous thing. I knew what could be done, and I *didn't* know which of those things I could do and which I couldn't.

The effect of Mars's gravity wasn't really being felt yet.

When it was, the ship would swing into position to blast against it.

"I don't see any ships coming out to help us," said Sammy, as we looked at the world that was to be our home or our grave.

"Write that off, Sammy," I said. "Take us as being the average ship. The average lifeship won't get any help—only the lucky ones."

"I thought we were supposed to be one of the lucky ones," said Sammy, with a grin. Sammy was like that—if others were optimistic, he was gloomy; if others were gloomy, he was cheerful.

"So we are lucky. Here we are, heading straight for Mars, taken all the way by three minutes' blast from Earth. That's luck. Nobody could count on it. But on the other hand, it's not by any means fantastic or incredible, considering that's precisely what they were planning for every lifeship, back on Earth, for months. I mean, if you aim for a clay pipe at a fairground and ring a gold watch, that's blind luck. But if you aim carefully for the gold watch, and get it, that's——"

"I get your point. So we're not going to get any help?"

"Doesn't look like it. And it doesn't look at all likely that we're going to orbit, either. The course was too good. If we were going to miss Mars we might be captured by it—but we're not."

"That leaves us to try for orbit or landing. Which is it going to be?"

"Landing," I said promptly.

Sammy raised his eyebrows. "Isn't the other the better chance?"

"Yes. But if we fail to orbit, we lose the chance to try to land soft. If we try to land . . . well, we certainly land. Depends how hard, that's all."

I had thought there would be all sorts of last-minute things to do, things to clear up. But I found myself suddenly, without warning, talking to everyone in the lounge and telling them the trip was over bar the question of success or failure.

122

"I never told you why I slammed on the acceleration when we were coming unstuck," I said, and there was sudden attention that I hadn't quite had until then. When I began to speak, they probably thought it was just Bill talking to them, not Lieutenant Easson. "I saw we weren't going to have enough fuel, and I tried to save some. You knew when Jim went to that other ship that he was looking for fuel, but I didn't say then that under no circumstances could the fuel I had land us safely on Mars."

"We guessed that, son," said Harry. "Bad news travels fast. I think we all knew. But thanks all the same. It was a nice thought."

I looked around at them. Yes, nobody seemed surprised. Betty was clutching Morgan tightly, as though, if they were close enough together, nothing could harm them. Leslie was playing with Bessie, and though I knew she was listening intently to what was going on, she showed no sign of it. Stowe nodded slowly, and clasped Caroline's hand. Jim couldn't help looking rather disappointed that everyone knew what he had been carefully guarding as a secret.

"Well, that saves a lot of trouble," I said briskly. "All right, get strapped up now and into your couches and be patient. I'm going to wait until I think the time's right, and then blast with all we've got in the way that gives us the best chance."

I looked at them intently. "It'll be cruel," I warned them. "Far worse than when we left Earth. You'll feel the floor's trying to push its way right through you. Don't think you have to bear it silently. Scream all you like—it'll help."

"How many Gs will it be, Lieutenant Bill?" asked Jim, interested.

"I don't know, Jim. I'll tell you this—it'll be more than the human frame is supposed to be able to stand. But that's something that's been put up time and again. Let's see if we can put it up once more. People who traveled at twelve miles an hour didn't have their heads blown off, remember."

"Will the linings stand it?" Jim asked.

I made a face at him. "Think about that after we land,

Jim," I told him. "Just at the moment, please keep that and any other interesting questions to yourself."

"How long have we got?" asked Sammy.

"Plenty of time, I suppose, but better start strapping each other up now. There may not be as much time as I think."

Imprex was developed primarily for this job. It's a binding tape that sticks only to itself, easily torn off when there's no strain, and stronger and stronger as the strain is put on it. It's elastic and equalizes the strain against it throughout its length. For support against acceleration or deceleration, it's better than anything else.

I waited in the control room while Leslie helped the others, then came back to strap her up myself. That was the only time on the trip that Leslie got special consideration from me. I wanted to be sure that she was as well prepared to stand the deceleration as she could be.

She wanted to be with me in the control room, but we couldn't shift her couch in there. I taped her very carefully, probing delicately at the imprex and taking it off again if it was a fraction too tight or too loose.

"None of the others are done as carefully as this," Leslie whispered. "Shouldn't I . . . ?"

"It won't make all that difference," I said. "But while I've got a certain responsibility to you all, I feel I have a special responsibility for my wife."

Now I couldn't see Mars any more. It was beneath our jets as the ship dropped. I was letting it drop.

Mars had an air pressure of between six and seven pounds —quite enough for life on a world that called for little effort. Since there wasn't any air until much nearer the surface, my altimeter was useless. I didn't know, couldn't know, exactly where we were in relation to Mars. My calculations were based on a constant speed, and checked by Phobos and Deimos, which I could see.

I had known all along that it was liable to be like this— blasting for a short time, too little, too late. There had been no dramatic last-minute rescue. None of us had been able to construct a superdrive out of the sole of a shoe and a couple of hairpins. We didn't, unfortunately, carry an amateur Einstein who was able to work out on the back of an envelope a way of landing safely without using any fuel at all.

Far from all this, what it came to in the end was that I sat with my hand poised over the firing button, waiting till it felt right to close it.

I've known men who trusted their lives to their instinct for the right moment. They did it because they had found it paid off. I only did it because I had to.

Now, I thought, and closed the switch. There was no sound. There was nothing outside for the blast to thunder against.

But I didn't miss sound in the welter of tortured vision, crushing gravity, drumming in my brain, and shooting pains. It was much worse than I had expected, worse than I had been able to imagine. My teeth ached, there was a fire in my belly, someone seemed to be tearing my skin off with pincers. There were sensations that I couldn't explain afterward.

It was a thousand tortures all at once. I remembered reading that some worlds were so dense that a steel bar would flow like liquid. I felt like the steel bar. I felt as if I was on the point of collapsing into the constituent elements of my body, but something was stubbornly holding me together to suffer more.

I never thought of the others below suffering the same thing. There comes a point when nothing exists but one's own pain—it shuts out the rest of the universe.

I clung at first to the idea that this couldn't last long. Soon, however, I had to give that up. To the creature I had been before I started the blast, a few seconds were a mere breath of existence. But now every instant was an eternity of agony.

I was actually praying for the last dregs of fuel to be used up and the deceleration to stop. Instead of wishing we had more fuel I wished we had less and that the ordeal would be over.

I watched the dials every millimeter of the way. I split their remaining traverse into imaginary divisions, so that I could tell myself: *Now there's only a quarter to go. An eighth. A sixteenth. A thirty-second* . . .

I prepared myself for the awful moment of helplessness I'd been anticipating the whole trip—the moment when the drive stopped and the ship went on and I couldn't do a thing about it. I was both dreading it and waiting impatiently for it. When the needles touched the mark my impatience for the ordeal to be over had almost won, and I tried to draw in a breath of thankfulness.

But it didn't come, for though the instruments said the fuel was finished—the blast went on.

I looked around the dials again, thinking that under the strain I had miscalculated. There wasn't a simple 30-20-10-0 type of gauge—you had to balance two or three things to calculate the actual quantity of fuel left. I was still right. There was *no* fuel left.

And the drive still went on.

So there was a safety margin. After all, there might be enough. In one blinding instant I experienced every emotion I had ever experienced in my life. There was wild hope that we were going to be safe after all. There was fury that we had been tricked, that all my calculations had been ruined by this revelation that there had been something in reserve. There was an apathetic desire that we would crash and die and it would all be over. There was misery, self-pity, regret, disgust, fear.

Everything that was in me was being squeezed out. I was an organ on which every stop was out, every note sounding together in shattering cacophony. I realized that if I lived through this any horror that ever happened to me subsequently would be a pale ghost beside it—but that thought was swept away by the passionate conviction that no one, nothing, could live through this. I was dead, we were all dead, squirming in our last agony like a crushed insect.

And then, unexpectedly, came a blessed release. The torture went on, but it suddenly seemed unimportant. I could think again. I could wonder whether the extra fuel was a mere accident, the result of faulty equipment on the lifeship, or if it was a deliberately concealed reserve which every lifeship had, a safety margin to turn the impossible into the just barely possible. I could think of Leslie and hope fervently that what had happened to Mary Stowe hadn't happened to her. I could marvel that our rocket linings had stood the strain. I could think gleefully of what I might, after all, be able to say to Sammy about whether we had been lucky or not.

And just as I realized that the thousand-to-one chance had swelled and swelled until it threatened to explode, we crashed. I had time to appreciate no more than the fact that we were down, when I bounced out of the couch as if I'd fallen on it from a great height, and smashed the dials in front of me with my face.

When I became conscious again, two things registered at once, jamming each other. There was gravity; and I couldn't see. For a second or two they fought with each other, then a feeling of peace and relief flowed over me.

Even before I knew I wasn't blind, I realized that I'd much rather be alive and blind than not alive at all. So it was with real pleasure that I found that even through closed eyelids and bandages I could see light. It must be bright. This was Mars, lit by the new, brighter sun.

I moved, and though I was sore all over it was quite a pleasant soreness—like rest after long, back-breaking labor. My arms, my legs, my head, everything moved. I was in bed, and the sheets were cool.

"Leslie," I said. I don't know how I knew she was there, but I did. I drew my arms clear of the sheets, ignoring the stiffness, reached out—and Leslie was in them.

"Bill," she whispered. I sensed her bending over me, and her lips brushed mine lightly. I felt her anxiously. She had an arm in a sling, but as far as her knees I couldn't feel anything else wrong.

"No, I'm all right," she said. "So are you, except for perhaps a scar or two that'll make you look distinguished."

For long seconds we just held each other. But then I had to ask:

"How many of us are safe?"

She laughed breathlessly. "All," she said. "Every one. Sammy, Harry, Bessie, Morgan, Betty, the Stowes. And you and me. The lifeship didn't come through too well, but . . ."

"The other ships?" I demanded. "How many of them are getting through?"

"Hundreds," she said lightly. "They're dropping all over Mars. Most of them are dropping too hard, though. Don't think of that now, Bill. We don't know the picture yet. We don't know how many lifeships are going to land safely, but you were right enough—it can only be one out of quite a lot."

She laughed again, and I felt her lay her cheek against my bandaged face.

"Still, with you piloting the ship, how could we help but be the one?"

One Too Many

1

"You and I ought to be friends, Bill," said Alec Ritchie, in his usual good-humored tone, "because the two best-looking girls in what's left of the human race come and visit us."

I grinned involuntarily. "Is that a good reason?" I asked. "Anyway, I didn't know I was being unfriendly."

"You weren't," Ritchie said cheerfully, "but you don't like me and you make only halfhearted attempts to hide it."

I didn't answer that, because it was perfectly true.

Ritchie was one of those fortyish, stocky, even-tempered men who laugh a lot with their faces but never with their eyes, and whom hardly anyone ever does like very much. Lieutenant Porter was dead, killed in the lifeship crash that had broken Ritchie's leg, but he probably hadn't liked Ritchie either. Why he had chosen Ritchie and brought him to Mars was all too obvious. Ritchie's daughter Aileen was almost certainly one of the two most beautiful girls on Mars, just as he said.

Whether Leslie was the other I couldn't say. I was biased. Besides, I hadn't seen all the others. Neither had Ritchie, but he was evidently prepared to guess. I imagined he would always be ready to guess, particularly if there was any percentage in it. Coming to Mars would have made no difference to that.

Earth by this time was dead, boiled sterile. Ritchie and I were two of the few thousand lucky people who had not only got a place on one of the lifeships but had also landed safely on Mars. Fairly safely, anyway.

And Mars?

Take one small, moribund planet, cold, dry, brittle, dark, and cheerless. Turn on spit for two months, one complete turn every twenty-four and a half hours. Serve piping hot to fourteen thousand hungry and uncritical guests just in from space.

And don't blame any remarks they may make on Emily Post.

When all that extra heat from the new, brighter sun first hit Mars, practically all the water on the planet, whether it was ice, liquid, or mixed with the dust of erosion in the dull, bodiless mud of Mars, had been lifted right up into the atmosphere. A lot of the dust went with it. There were black clouds, sandstorms, dust storms, and, as soon as the particle-laden water vapor hit streams of colder air, torrents of muddy rain. It couldn't have been an altogether pleasant time for the seven thousand people who had been on Mars at the time —the colony which had existed before the big migration became necessary.

But at that time I had been mainly concerned with getting

my lifeship and the ten people in it to Mars, whatever the conditions there were like. That was enough to worry about without looking for more.

Well, I'd done that. That worry was over. Now all I wanted to do was stay in bed for twenty years or so, smiling modestly when people came to visit me and tell me what a magnificent job I'd done.

Sammy came to visit me and told me: "You've been swinging the lead long enough, Bill. While you still had those bandages over your eyes there might have been some excuse, but now it's high time you stopped malingering and started earning your keep."

Behind me, Ritchie laughed uproariously. "That's telling him," he spluttered happily.

"This is a private discussion, mister," said Sammy coldly. "Bill's a friend of mine. We've been through a lot. We understand each other. If we did happen to want your opinion, we'd ask for it."

Sammy clearly didn't like Ritchie either. Ritchie merely laughed again. He never lost his temper.

"Where's Leslie?" I asked Sammy.

"She's working, pinhead. Don't you know yet only one can get away from the job at a time? Work Party No. 94 can't spare two people to come and hold your hand, even if you are pretending to be dying."

"What's the job you're doing?"

"Digging holes," said Sammy succinctly.

"And filling them in again?" I asked, because that seemed to be the implication.

"No, we don't have to do that. The wind does it for us."

"Who's in charge?"

"Of the whole show, or just 94?"

In the hospital we didn't know much about the general situation. No one had time to explain it to us.

"You tell me, Sammy," I suggested, "taking it I know but nothing."

"You don't have to tell me that," Sammy assured me. "You

always were an ignorant cuss. Well, such government as there is at the moment is on the additive principle. You know, you start with a hut, build two rooms onto it, then a corridor all around, then an east wing, then a hall, a west wing, some more corridors and an annex, all carefully planned so that every time you want to go to the lavatory you have to go up and down six flights of stairs and walk three miles along passages.

"Viz—the original colony had its own administration, of course, and when the big spaceships got here the top brass added themselves onto that, and when the lifeships arrived the lieutenants were added onto *that*, so that now——"

He interrupted himself and asked belligerently: "Do you follow that, or can't you understand a simple explanation?"

I grinned. "Now tell me who's in charge of 94."

"Me, until they throw you out of here. Leslie, when I'm not around."

"So I'm still the boss, am I?"

"I wouldn't say that, but you're still supposed to take the rap for anything that goes wrong, if that's what you mean. Lifeship crews are staying together as units, lieutenants in charge. Sometimes a work party wants a different lieutenant, or a lieutenant wants a different work party, and there's a switch. But that isn't happening often."

"Surprising," I commented, "but good to hear all the same."

"You mean, Sammy," said Ritchie from the next bed, "that as far as the work parties are concerned these so-called lieutenants are still the little tin gods—no chance for anyone else to step in and run things? No offense, Bill."

Sammy turned a cold eye on Ritchie again. "I thought I told you this was a private discussion," he observed. "And my name's Hoggan."

"Pleased to meet you," said Ritchie affably. "My name's Ritchie."

Sammy's sense of humor almost got the better of him. He

nearly laughed. He was hard put to it to remember he didn't like Ritchie and retort bluntly: "All right, Ritchie. You have my permission to exist. But do it quietly, will you? I want to talk to Bill."

"Go ahead," said Ritchie airily.

Sammy stared at him for a moment, then turned back to me. "Seriously," he said, "there isn't much need for government just now, and by the time we do need it there'll be something better. On the whole, things would be all right but for—Holy Moses, what's this?"

We looked around at a sudden uproar of whistles and wolf calls from the other men in the ward. Sammy hadn't heard it before, but I had. It meant Leslie or Aileen had just come in.

This time it was Leslie. She hurried along the ward, paying no attention to the chorus of approbation, and stopped at the foot of my bed.

"I need you, Sammy," she said breathlessly, ignoring me. "It's Morgan again."

"What's he doing now?" Sammy sighed, hoisting himself up in a way that showed how glad he must have been to sit down.

"It's what he's not doing," she told him. "I've done all I can, with no result. Now you'll have to come and clout his ear."

"You might have done that yourself, without bothering me," Sammy grumbled. "Surely you didn't let a little thing like that stop you?"

"That" was the sling supporting her right arm.

"Frankly, I did," said Leslie. "Morgan's looking ugly." She took a couple of quick steps, bent over, and pecked me briefly on the cheek. There was uproar in the ward again. Then she hustled Sammy out. Apart from that quick peck she hadn't even glanced at me.

And odd though it might seem, I was pleased. I hadn't thought Leslie was going to be as businesslike and brisk and good at handling people as it seemed she was. I should have known, I suppose. She had been a schoolteacher, and handling twenty to thirty boisterous kids was probably good practice for handling a work party.

So Morgan Smith was giving trouble again, which meant he had been giving trouble before.

"Who's this fellow who's making a nuisance of himself?" asked Ritchie curiously.

"Morgan Smith. Why?"

"Oh, sometimes it's useful to know about people who make a nuisance of themselves."

I grunted and went back to my thoughts.

Morgan had been a gamble, but so had they all. I had known all along the risk that some of the men and women I chose, instead of being the people who most deserved to live, would be the people above all who should have been left behind.

Sammy hadn't been serious, I knew, when he said I was malingering, but when I looked around the ward it seemed that everyone else there was so much more seriously hurt than I was that it was high time I was up and earning my keep, as Sammy said. Besides, if there was any strong-arm stuff to be done in my work party, I should be the one to do it. Sammy was tough enough, but slightly built. Leslie, normally, could look after herself, but not with a broken ulna. John Stowe and Harry Phillips were much older than Morgan. I was the only one so much stronger and tougher than Morgan that he'd be ill advised to give me any trouble.

No one seemed to be asleep. I bellowed: "Nurse!"

She appeared at once, a rather hard-faced woman who had once, I believed, been matron of a big London hospital. When she saw who had called for her she frowned. We knew she had three other wards to look after. We weren't supposed to bother her more than we could help, and people like me weren't supposed to bother her at all.

"I know you're busy, Nurse," I said. "I just want to remove myself from your charge. Seems there's trouble in my work party, and . . ."

"Lieutenant," she said wearily, "there's trouble in every work party. People don't like working fourteen hours a day. When you join your group, you'll have to give orders, and you'll have to be fit."

"I know, but . . ."

"People who can't take orders generally aren't very good at giving them. Wait till the doctor sees you. When he says you can go, you'll go."

She didn't wait to hear what I had to say to this, but made her way out of the ward again.

"That seems to be that," said Ritchie.

I ignored him.

Now that I knew I had to stay where I was, I was even more impatient to get out of the hospital. Things were going on; Mars was being reshaped, my ex-crew, now Work Party 94, was working on a job, and I wasn't with them.

The rain started again soon after that. Considering how little water there was on Mars, compared with Earth, it was astonishing what the planet could do with it. I hadn't seen the rain yet, for there were no windows in our ward, but I'd heard it. Often.

None of us in the ward knew at first hand what conditions outside were like, for the recent history of all of us was the same. We had all been injured in lifeship landings on Mars, and brought straight to the hospital.

This time the rain sounded worse than usual. I wasn't surprised when Leslie came back and the whistles sounded again.

Men are like that. Some of the patients in the ward were pretty badly smashed up, but show them an attractive girl and they'd holler and whistle, just to show they weren't dead yet. Even those who moaned and whined and tossed about at other times made a gallant effort to look happy and well when Leslie or Aileen was in the ward. That sort of thing could give you a lump in the throat if you let it.

"We've knocked off for a bit," Leslie told me, sitting on the bed. There was nowhere else to sit. "We couldn't do anything. We can hardly see." She sighed. "I'll be glad when you're back, Bill."

"I tried to get out of here but was slapped down. What exactly is the trouble, Leslie? What's wrong?"

She pulled herself together and smiled brightly—the too quick smile of so many women when the last thing they feel like doing is smiling. "Oh, nothing really," she said. "Don't bother about it now. Just get well, Bill, and don't worry. We'll be all right."

"Tell me," I insisted.

She hesitated, then it all came out in a rush. "It's not one thing, Bill. It's about a hundred things, all piling up. It's the rain, and the winds, and the dust, and the heat. Sand and dust in everything, grit in your mouth and eyes and hair. It's the work—digging out foundations for buildings, and the wind filling them with sand and dust. Everybody grumbling, saying the same things over and over again. It's trying to sleep in a corridor, packed like sardines, with the sweat running all over you."

She tried to stop, but the words came pouring out of her. "Then there's the food, things you can't identify, things that taste like string. No milk. No coffee. No eggs. No meat. No hot drinks, because water boils when it's lukewarm. Washing in muddy water, because we've only enough clean water for drinking and cooking.

"Everybody coming to you with their troubles. Betty afraid that with all this work she's going to lose her baby. Little Bessie always in the way. Jim working far too hard, the only one we have to stop working sometimes. People from other crews trying to drag us into their quarrels. Back-breaking days that go on and on and on until you really believe there's never going to be an end to them, though you're so tired your brain's buzzing. Being hot, cold, drenched, parched, tired, and restless, all within an hour or so. Oh, I could scream!"

"Don't scream here," I said, "but cry if you like—you might enjoy that better than screaming."

"I expect so," Leslie said moodily, "but you need training to cry in front of all these people, and I haven't got it. Anyway, there's all that, and Morgan."

"Yes?" I said. "What about Morgan?"

"Morgan's a kind of last straw. I don't really mind the weather or the food or sleeping with nineteen other women, because no one can do anything about it. And the work's got to be done. There can't be any improvements until we've put up more buildings, grown more crops, and all the rest of it. But Morgan . . ."

"Well, what's he doing?" I asked a little impatiently.

She shook her head. "Wait till you see for yourself."

"Why the mystery? If he's a nuisance, he must be doing something. What is it?"

"Just being a heel," said Leslie, "in every possible, conceivable way. He's making Betty's life hell, though the poor kid tries to hide it. Whatever he ought to do, he does the exact opposite. No, I knew I couldn't describe it so you'd understand. You'll know soon enough."

She looked up as Aileen came in to see Ritchie. She and Aileen nodded to each other.

"You know her?" I murmured.

"She's in 92, working near us. And she's one of the nineteen women I sleep with. After eight hours crushed up against someone, you feel you know her."

I grinned. "I know it's easy for me to be cheerful," I said, "but is everything really as black as all that? Just look back. On Earth all that mattered was getting a place on a lifeship. People would have given anything for that."

"I know," she said gloomily. "You needn't remind me how I tried to bribe you."

She must really be feeling low if she took it that way. I pretended she hadn't said anything.

"Then when we were on the lifeship," I went on quickly, "we just wanted to get safely to Mars. Nothing else mattered. Even if we'd been told about this, we'd have thought it was heaven. Now we're here, and in no immediate danger any more, yet we're——"

"I know," she said, still in the same gloomy tone. "We're waiting for something worse. At least, I am. Can you blame me, Bill? All along we've thought—if only we get through this all right, everything will be wonderful. And it never is."

"When something like this happens," I said quietly, "no one has any right to think things are going to be wonderful. You have to be satisfied just to be alive. After a big smack like this, things even out only gradually. You've got to be patient."

I grinned again. "It's just as well I know you, Leslie, or I'd be doing you an injustice. You're only unloading all this on me because you've been cheerfully accepting everything that everybody else unloaded on you. You feel you ought to have a chance to moan about things too."

She smiled despite herself. "There may be something in that. Oh, damn, hear that? I think the rain's off. I'll have to go back."

She stood up straight with an effort. "Hurry and come back, Bill," she said. "I miss you."

"That's nice," I said. "But do it with moderation. Don't miss me too much."

Aileen didn't go when Leslie did. Apparently it was Aileen's rest period. With Leslie gone, I looked idly at Aileen, who was talking quietly with Ritchie.

She was certainly a good-looking girl, rather like Leslie in some ways. They were both blondes for a start, Aileen very light, Leslie a deeper gold. Neither of them was the model type. They both had the slim waist and long, slender legs of a model, but they didn't have the exaggeration of breast and hip. They both looked intelligent—in fact, intelligent rather than pretty. And they moved with the same lithe assurance.

The redheaded youth across from me kept trying to catch Aileen's eye and making mildly erotic gestures. That sort of thing never bothered Leslie, but it was obviously annoying Aileen. I heard her murmur to Ritchie: "So help me, I'm going to blister that character's ears on my way out." Ritchie chuckled.

I noticed that Aileen and Ritchie never touched each other. Her manner toward him was more that of a rather nervous secretary than of a loving daughter.

When at last Aileen rose to go, she looked across at the red-haired youth, obviously intending to go over and tell him what she thought of him.

"Aileen!" I said sharply.

She turned, a little startled. She had never spoken to me. But when I beckoned she came and bent over me.

"He's going to die tonight or tomorrow night," I said quietly.

She straightened abruptly. "Oh," she said, and her face went pink. "Thanks for telling me—Lieutenant Easson, isn't it?"

I nodded. She walked away along the ward. She must have flashed a friendly smile at the redhead, from the reaction of the other men in the ward, but as her back was to me I didn't see it.

Ritchie grinned. "Why did you have to spoil it?" he asked playfully. "Why didn't you let her blister his ears and *then* find out?"

I frowned. "You think that would have been funny?" I asked incredulously.

"Yes. But then, I've been told I have a peculiar sense of humor."

"You have," I told him, and pointedly looked away. I heard Ritchie chuckle, meaninglessly.

The doctor wouldn't clear me that day, or the next. The day after that I was given my clothes and told I could go, but to take it easy.

The way it was said made it clear that it was said from habit, not because the doctor thought I *would* take it easy, or that anyone could afford to nurse himself with things as they were.

141

Before I went, when it was known I was going, Ritchie made me a proposition.

"Ever struck you, Bill, that this is the greatest chance ever for smart businessmen?" he asked.

"What is?"

"The setup here. Rebuilding. Starting again. It's better than getting in on the ground floor. It's a chance to move into the basement."

"Money doesn't exist any more," I said shortly, a little disgusted at the idea of making capital out of mankind's greatest disaster.

Ritchie shrugged his heavy shoulders. "What's money? All that ever mattered was what you could get for it. This is a chance to get it. Now, you're still a lieutenant, Bill. You have power, and any little piece of power you have is a chance to get more. If you and I work together, starting not when it's too late, but right now——"

"Not interested," I said flatly. I was going to say more, angrily, but Ritchie's smooth, pleasant voice cut in.

"Listen, Bill, I understand your idealism. I like you for it. But don't you see what's going to happen? If you're not ambitious, someone else will be. You want to make Mars a safe place, a good place. Fine. And while you're doing it someone will be building himself up so that when you've made Mars a safe place, a good place, he'll be able to step in and take it from you."

I stared at him.

"I'm not suggesting," said Ritchie earnestly, "that you *shouldn't* work for the good of everybody. Of course you will. But don't forget, while you're doing it, that human beings aren't perfect. Don't forget that you can't rely on everyone to be as honest and unselfish and idealistic as you. Look after your interests—no one else will. Come in with me, help me, and you and I will——"

"You're making quite a lot of sense," I said, "but the answer's still no. Build your own empire, Ritchie."

"All right," said Ritchie evenly. "I will."

142

So before I was even out of the hospital I should have been pretty well prepared for the many battles which I knew were coming. I knew about Mars, though not at first hand. I knew about the people who were trying to make it a world fit to live in. I knew about Morgan Smith. And I knew about Alec Ritchie. I wouldn't have had to be much of a prophet to have a general picture of what was going to happen.

I wasn't much of a prophet. Or I didn't think. What happened hardly ever found me better prepared than anyone else.

2

When I came out of the hospital, alone, I stood still for a long time at the door and just looked around me.

This was the future home of the human race—now and for a long time to come. Mercury, Venus, and Earth would be too hot for human beings for millions of years. Science would have to advance about twice as far as it had already come from zero before Jupiter or any of the other outer planets could be forced to provide a comfortable environment for mankind. There would be little settlements, undoubtedly, on asteroids and satellites. But now and for untold generations Mars was the only place for men and women to live.

That made grumbles about the world itself absolutely pointless. It was now of purely academic interest that there had once been a world on which water boiled at 100° C.

If the pre-space-travel calculations had been correct and Mars had had an atmosphere too thin and with too little oxygen to support human life, human life would simply have ceased to exist when the sun underwent its change. As it was, we could only be thankful that Mars had just enough air, water, and whatever else we needed to enable us to live fairly comfortably on it until we were once more in a position to take command of our environment.

That wouldn't be soon. We had left a highly mechanized culture back on Earth, but it would be some time before we had climbed to the same point on Mars. For a year or two at least things would be very primitive. Hydroelectric power was out of the question, and the use of oil, gasoline, or coal for generating electricity was just as impracticable. We simply had to use the new source of power, the one we didn't know very much about—atomic power.

That meant that there would be plenty of power when we had any at all.

Nuclear physics had come a long way since the time when the power of the atom could only be used to make a big bang. But it hadn't come anywhere near the beautiful simplicity of really efficient technology. Atom power was still huge, clumsy, and uncertain.

None of the spaceships was atom-powered. It was a pity, in a way, that such a wonder fuel as moluone had been discovered, back in the fifties. Instead of having to plug away at atomic power to make space travel possible, the interplanetary pioneers had turned their backs on it, since they didn't need it, and now we had to start from scratch. Moluone was a wonder fuel for space travel, all right, but it was no earthly use for ground-based industry. If there had been just one experimental atom-powered ship, it might have saved twenty thousand people ten years of toil.

I sighed and moved away from the door of the research station. People were going in and coming out, and I was in the way. Nobody paid any attention to me, apart from a few people who glanced curiously at my uniform, as if they had never seen such a thing before.

Nobody else was wearing anything like my uniform, certainly. Every other person I saw, of either sex, wore a sort of smock, except a few men who wore only shorts. The improvised garment which was so generally worn was like shorts and a sleeveless shirt except that it was in one piece. If existing shorts and shirts were used, they were sewn together at the waist. So far I didn't know why. There was seldom any attempt, even in the case of the women, to make the one-piece suits attractive. There were none with halter tops or bare backs or low necklines. They were plain and strong and simple. But of course the girls who were attractive looked attractive anyway.

I made my way slowly to where Party 94 was working. I'd been told where to go. No one around had so little to do that he had time to come and show me the way. As I went I continued my first survey of the Martian scene.

There had been a colony of about seven thousand people on Mars before the disaster. That didn't seem many now, but it had been a lot when Mars was a dead world, a mere research station for astronomers, physicists, metallurgists, geologists, archaeologists, botanists, and scores of other ists.

With all the people that the regular spaceships and the lifeships had been able to bring from the doomed Earth in the time available, there still weren't many more than twenty thousand people on Mars, including all the ists.

From the short-term point of view, it was just as well that there weren't any more. The fact that there had been permanent accommodation for seven thousand people for a start meant that there was some sort of temporary accommodation for the whole twenty thousand.

146

The settlement had been called Winant, after the first man to land on Mars, and it looked as if the town that was going to grow up around it would be called Winant too. So many people had so many different ideas about what to call the first Martian township that the easiest way out of the impasse seemed to be to use the existing name.

The Winant scene was typical of all Mars. The sun was bright, surrounded and diffused by a strong haze. Mars would always have a lot of dust in the atmosphere. It was warm but not unbearably hot; the air generally was so dry that people could be comfortable at much higher temperatures than could have been borne on Earth. The smaller effort that the reduced gravity called for was another thing that made the heat bearable.

The sky was deep, luminous blue—deeper than it had ever been on Earth. The ground was colorful, though flat and almost featureless—red, yellow, green, and brown. Most of the rocks near the surface had been worn long ago into sand and dust. But here and there were little ridges of rock and stone, eroded to mere remnants of the mountains they must once have been.

Mars hadn't had an earthquake for millions of years. The ground surface was very much as it must have been in the time of the first Cro-Magnon on Earth. There was nothing much to see on Mars itself—there never was. The only native form of life was plant life, lichen and a few varieties of moss. There was plenty of that.

Anything of interest had to be supplied by the people from Earth. Around Winant there was plenty. First there were the long, flat buildings of the research station, built not for this new Mars but for the cold, dark, sterile world Mars had been before the sun stepped up its output. There were hardly any windows.

All around the station buildings were piles of equipment, stones, metal from broken-up lifeships, stores of all kinds— mostly fastened down firmly so that the gales, of which there was no sign at present, couldn't scatter them all over the land-

147

scape. Drawn up behind the station were about a hundred lifeships, being used for temporary accommodation. Behind them again were the larger spaceships, the ships that had been in existence before the emergency was known.

Among the ships were corralled the cattle which had been brought from Earth. It seemed crazy to bring cattle to Mars instead of human beings, but unless such provision had been made we would have had to manage henceforth without meat, milk, leather, and wool. As it was, we had none of these things at the moment; we couldn't allow the cattle to breed until we had fodder for them. They ate the sparse Martian lichen, but it wasn't enough. They needed Earth-type grass, which was only now being introduced to Mars.

In front of the station, about a hundred yards from it, thousands of people were engaged on what looked already like vast excavations. We had heard blasting frequently in the hospital.

I stopped a tall girl who was on her way toward the huge hole in the rock. "What's going on there?" I asked.

Miraculously, even here she was chewing something. It couldn't be gum; there wasn't any.

"Just out of the hospital, Lieutenant?" she said in the well-remembered accents of Brooklyn. "You want to know what we're doing? We're digging out a cliff face. When we've got it, we're going to dig caves in it. Now I got to run."

"Thanks," I said.

"You're welcome," said Brooklyn.

There was more sense in it than appeared at first. We could live on the surface, but we wanted greater atmospheric pressure if we could get it. We *could* get it, by digging for it. A mile or two down, conditions would be appreciably nearer what we were used to. Besides, long ago our ancestors had found that caves made very comfortable houses. Dig a hole in a perpendicular face of rock, find some way of closing it behind you, and you have a very fair house.

But I had spent long enough getting my bearings in this new world. I picked my way among the piles of material in search of Work Party 94. I was lightheaded, stiff, a little uncertain on my feet, and had a dull ache in my temples. But in what proportion my lightheadedness was owing to the light air pressure of Mars and to my convalescence I didn't know. My lungs weren't troubled at all. There was slightly more oxygen in the Martian mixture than there had been in the Terran variety of air. Some of it had been released recently by the extra heat warming the many surface oxides.

When I found 94 I didn't have time for any greetings. Harry Phillips, Caroline and Jim Stowe turned and saw me. They didn't show any sign of welcome, only of relief.

Harry said: "Son, I think you'd better get around the back fast."

"What's the matter?"

"If I were you I wouldn't waste any time finding out."

I didn't. "Around the back" was behind a stone wall about ten feet high. I was still unsteady, but on Mars I could run. I did run.

Morgan had his back to me. I could see Leslie's face over his shoulder, but not, at first, what he was doing. She didn't see me either. She was scared.

Then I saw Morgan was picking and pulling and jabbing at her injured arm, holding her other wrist so that she couldn't get away. He wasn't so much hurting her as trying to frighten her, and in that he was succeeding very well.

I didn't rush in at once. I waited until I was quite sure what was going on, and that Morgan wasn't merely defending himself against some ill-considered attack by Leslie, and until I was good and mad. Then I stepped forward, swung Morgan around, and planted my fist hard on his nose. What happened was more of a surprise to me than to him.

I had grown used to the light gravity of Mars but hadn't had much opportunity to learn all its effects. With the force of the blow Morgan and I staggered away from each other. Morgan was the one who was unlucky. His foot caught on a stone and he went over hard, the force of his fall being

149

caused more by his momentum than by gravity. I saw he was out and turned to Leslie.

"Where's Sammy?" I demanded.

"At the stores." She pushed back her disheveled hair and straightened herself abruptly as if to shake the fright out of herself. "He can't always be around. Glad to see you, Bill."

"Has this sort of thing happened often?"

She shrugged. "All the time, more or less. Not that exactly, but something like it."

"But why don't the rest of you gang up on Morgan?"

She shrugged again. "We have, occasionally. He always gets his own back. So generally we don't."

I exploded. "For heaven's sake! Morgan's just a cheap would-be tough guy. He can't build himself up into a menace unless you let him."

"Not," said Leslie patiently, "if you happen to be stronger than he is. We're not."

"Two of you are."

"If there're two around. You don't know much about the ordinary, typical child bully, do you, Bill? I do. He doesn't do anything when he isn't going to get away with it. Little Jimmy comes home crying, and Johnny gets a beating. Next day Johnny takes it out of little Jimmy. And this time little Jimmy knows better than to come home crying and blame it on Johnny. That's Morgan—a naughty boy, cruel, selfish, and petty, grown up physically but not mentally. He likes people to be afraid of him. He has to show he's the boss. He——"

I shook my head brusquely. "If that's all we'll soon knock it out of him."

"There speaks," said Leslie ironically, "the bigger and stronger boy."

"I don't say you can beat consideration for others into someone who doesn't have any. But you can make him toe the line, and that's what Morgan will have to do."

"All right," said Leslie with a wry grin. "You try it."

"I will," I said. "Better have a look and make sure he hasn't broken his skull."

"I sincerely hope he has."

Morgan came to as we looked at him. His eyes burned at me. He didn't have to say anything. His look spoke his hate.

"Watch your step, Morgan," I warned him. "From what I hear it's no good appealing to your better nature. So I'll just say the next time I find you stepping out of line I'll beat the hell out of you. Now get back to work."

"Work!" he exclaimed, his voice quivering with impotent resentment. Blood was streaming from his nose and he nursed his ankle theatrically. "How can I——"

"That's for you to find out," I said dispassionately. "If you're not up in five seconds I'll kick you in the ribs."

He was up and around the other side of the storage pile well inside the five seconds, limping dramatically but moving quickly all the same.

"That may be the way to treat him," Leslie admitted. "If he's scared of you, you may be able to handle him. But don't count on it. I've had twisted kids—the more you beat Johnny, the more he had to beat little Jimmy. If you half killed Johnny, that was just too bad for little Jimmy."

"What's the answer?"

She shook her head. "There isn't an answer. At least, the only answer's in psychotherapy, and pretty well hidden at that."

"This time there was another answer," I said, frowning. "Not bringing Morgan along. I should have found it."

She'd been arguing with me, but at that she changed sides at once. "You couldn't know everything, Bill," she said warmly. "It's not your fault that Morgan——"

"If bringing Morgan here was a mistake," I said, "it was my mistake. We argued about this before, back on Earth, and we didn't agree then. You thought all the biggest, the best, the greatest, the cleverest people should come along. I thought——"

"You were right, Bill. You were supposed to pick ten decent, ordinary people, and Morgan looked like a decent, ordinary person."

I nodded, and we didn't say any more about the matter. But I went on thinking about it, as I went back with her and found where everybody was and what they were doing, and what I was supposed to do.

The disaster had been a great chance to build a really worth-while community. Back on Earth we'd always had the excuse that we couldn't destroy the criminals, the insane, the psychotics, and the weak-minded, and so we could never have a perfect community. When the disaster came, we lieutenants had had that chance. We could just quietly ignore the criminals, the insane, the psychotics, and the weak-minded, and make sure that if we didn't have saints we had at least eliminated the worst of the sinners. And I hadn't taken that chance, apparently.

Leslie obviously thought Morgan was bad through and through. I hoped she was wrong.

In a way, all Mars, the whole future of the human race, depended on the lieutenants' choice. Decent, reasonable people would build a decent, reasonable community—and it would go on being what it was at the start. The future isn't what happens to happen, remote, untouchable. The future is what we have now, what we do, what we want, what we are.

The future was Leslie, Sammy, the Austrian doctor at the hospital, Alec Ritchie, the gum-chewing girl from Brooklyn— and Morgan.

I hoped it was a good future. I wasn't going to judge Morgan on hearsay—even on what Leslie said. I would give him every chance.

However, from what I'd seen I could only hope that a future with Morgan in it would be a good future. I couldn't count on it.

3

Things for the most part went fairly smoothly. It's not worth detailing all the jobs Work Party 94 did; there were too many of them, and we rarely saw much of anyone. It was a pity the different work parties couldn't be taken into the planning more and given some over-all impression of the work they were helping to do. People work better when they have a clear purpose and a set goal.

But there was no time for explanations yet. It was a case of "Do this until I tell you to stop," "Carry all that stuff from here to there," "Dig here until someone comes and tells you what else to do," and after a long, backbreaking day of toil in which nothing obvious was accomplished, a hot, stuffy, restless night in one of the corridors at the research station.

The nights were worse than the days. As far as temperature was concerned, there was no happy medium. Outside, it was below freezing; inside, the ventilating system planned to cope with seven thousand people labored hopelessly in its efforts to supply fresh, clean, cool air for three times that number.

We split up at night. Sammy and Harry Phillips were in one of the annexes with no less than ninety-eight other single men. Bessie was in one children's dormitory, Jim Stowe in another—the best accommodation naturally went to growing children. Leslie's status had changed since I left the hospital. She and I, the Stowes, and three other couples shared a tiny room which had once been a reading room—but nobody had any time for reading any more. Betty and Morgan were with five other couples in another tiny room somewhere.

I wondered sometimes how the research station staff, the people who had been there before the disaster, felt about this invasion. In those early days I seldom met any of them to find out, or if I did I didn't know it. For now the state of all of us was the same—a pair of hands and an aching back—whether we had come in the spaceships or lifeships or had been there all the time.

The main difficulty about the building situation was that the prevailing conditions didn't allow of temporary housing at all. The gales would blow tents and huts away. Light, flimsy structures weighed so little that it didn't take much of a wind to tear them away from the loose surface of Mars. When a house was built, the first essential was a deep, strong foundation. There was clay lower down, but the surface was shifting sand or fine dust.

By this time, the people who had been there longer than we had were telling us, the weather was really beginning to settle down. Though it rained every day, they pointed out that at least it was fairly clean rain.

A lot of the dust was out of the atmosphere now, though there were strange, beautiful effects at sunset and sunrise. The gales were not quite so fierce as they had been at first, and there were hardly any whirlwinds any more. Mars, after all, had few mountains, which was a factor tending toward stability; the ground and the air above it were heated pretty evenly. There were occasional calm periods. Sometimes Mars was like California in June. But only sometimes.

I soon saw the reason for the simple one-piece garment that nearly everyone wore. I saw it on my first day in the open.

Leslie and I were checking stores. Suddenly it was raining. There was no warning at all. I looked quickly around for shelter.

"You don't shelter on Mars," Leslie told me. "Not from rain. It's the wind that drives us under cover."

It was undoubtedly true that by the time we reached shelter we'd be too wet to care. I wondered why I was so wet so quickly. Then I saw why. I looked inquiringly at Leslie.

She nodded. "The rain's almost horizontal," she said. "It often is."

With only two fifths of Earth's gravity and much the same wind velocity, the rain didn't so much pour down as sweep along like the wind. Used to Earth, you felt it was raining up at you. It made raincoats ridiculous. It went down your collar, up your legs, and in a matter of seconds you were as wet as if you'd plunged into a lake.

Leslie went on working unconcernedly. I was just about to make some comment when the rain stopped almost as quickly as it had begun. It had lasted only about three minutes.

It stands to reason that a wind following a rainstorm is a wet wind. It's blowing over wet ground, drying it, picking up water of evaporation.

Well, on Mars that doesn't follow. Conditions on Mars are so different from those of Earth that you have to forget all your weather lore and start again before you can predict anything. On Mars the wind wheels so often that if there's one thing you can be reasonably certain about, it's that you'll have a dry wind following rain. That is, a dry wind sweeping in from an angle.

About sixty seconds after the last drops of rain had fallen, Leslie's legs were dry. A few minutes later her clothes were only slightly damp.

"That's why you wear that outfit?" I asked. "It's loose and it dries quickly?"

"Oh no," she said. "You'll see the reason for that in a minute." She looked at my shirt and slacks and smiled faintly.

"It could be a reason," I said. "My pants are still wet at the knees."

It was half an hour before a real wind came. I staggered when it hit me. Leslie, who knew how to brace herself, wasn't visibly perturbed.

"We take cover now," she said calmly, "if we can. If not, we lie down."

We fought our way to the pile of stores where the others were huddled. All the way my trouser legs billowed and flapped like blankets left out in a storm. Twice the wind dragged my shirt out from under my waistband. It did it in little sharp tugs, an inch at a time. Before I could get my shirt to stay put I had to tighten my belt until it was cutting me in two.

"You see why we wear a one-piece suit?" said Leslie breathlessly, as we joined the other members of 94 in the shelter of two head-high walls at right angles.

It was obvious now. The only thing to wear in a swirling wind like that was something simple, strong, and molded to the body, something that didn't catch the wind and couldn't be torn open and off. My legs were tired with the effort of moving them. My pants had acted like sails.

"Where's Betty?" said Leslie suddenly, sharply. "Look, Bill —catch her!"

I was still pondering over the effects of a strong wind with

156

only two fifths Earth gravity to hold things down. I turned wildly, startled, not knowing what I was looking for.

Leslie and I were strong and had plenty of power in our legs. Betty wasn't and hadn't. She was a featherweight at best; in a wind like that she was utterly helpless.

When I turned she was about twenty yards away. A second later she was less than ten. Somehow she was keeping herself upright, looking as if she was running but really being swept before the wind like a straw.

I leaped out and caught her—and we nearly knocked ourselves senseless. It was like when I hit Morgan. Gravity seems almost nothing, but inertia is still the same as ever. If Betty had run into a wall at the speed she had been going, she could have killed herself. I was quite hard enough to knock the wind out of her.

"Thanks, Bill," she gasped. "Oh, I was scared!"

"How often have I told you," Morgan snapped, "to lie down and stay put when a wind like that starts?"

"I know, Morgan," said Betty penitently. "But I couldn't. I was——"

"Then you're not going to last long on this unprintable world," said Morgan.

I considered slapping his head for that, but decided against it. Morgan had never sworn before. It was apparently part and parcel of his new self-assertion that he had to do everything that would shock or hurt or irritate the people around him. I had to be careful what evidences of it I noticed, or I'd be nagging at him the whole time.

Sammy was quite prepared to comment, though. "That's funny," he said in a tone of mild surprise. "I thought you came from a good home, Morgan."

Morgan pretended not to hear him.

That was a fair sample of the Martian weather. What really caused its extreme volatility was the steady rotation of the planet and the absence of large, open tracts of water, which would heat and cool fairly slowly. The red desert and the air over it were heated to at least 90° Fahrenheit, then spun into darkness at something below zero. The days on Mars would always be hot, the nights freezing. There would always be winds sweeping and swirling from the twilight zone. That was permanent.

However, in about twenty years, we were told, much of the temporary climatic upheaval would be over and Mars would begin to settle down to a less violent, more comfortable existence.

That would be fine for our children.

Crops came up rapidly in the few areas of good soil. There was enough water and plenty of heat. If these had been the only things that were needed Mars would have been choked by the grain yield, despite the wind.

But crops also needed soil, something better than the sterile dust and sand which covered most of the surface of Mars. Where good earth existed the crops blazed up like ignited kerosene—not quite the grain we had known, for it had to adapt and be adapted to the new conditions, but still usable. There wasn't enough of this good soil, however. Half the people on Mars were kept busy on the land.

The other half were busy building. That was our job, for the most part.

Except for Morgan we had no personnel problems in 94.

As I expected, Leslie's worry and dissatisfaction disappeared with her responsibility. "Now you can do the worrying, Bill," she said cheerfully, "and I'll make the sympathetic, understanding remarks. But you don't worry, do you?"

"Not more than I can help," I said. "Leads to ulcers. And who wants ulcers?"

Yes, Leslie was a simple, straight-thinking, sunny character. She wasn't capricious or moody. I suppose I'd try to cover up Leslie's faults if she had any, but really there isn't any covering up to do. Back on Earth she hadn't always shown up too well, but that was when I didn't know her and she didn't know me. As we grew into each other's ways, it became almost impossible for us to have any serious disagreement, so long as I remembered—and I did—to tell Leslie every so often how much I loved her.

As for Sammy, he worked hard, made only the routine complaints, and didn't seem nearly so certain now that it would have been a good idea never to have been born.

"What's come over you, Sammy?" Leslie asked him once. "I haven't heard you prophesying disaster for weeks now. Did it take all the wind out of your sails when Bill got the lifeship down safely?"

Sammy grunted. "Mark my words," he said darkly, "there'll be dirty work or catastrophe or tragedy yet. I don't know what's going to happen, but something will."

Though he spoke with his own pessimistic brand of humor, it was clear that he half meant what he said.

"The leopard," Leslie sighed, "doesn't change his spots, I see. But I think I know what's the trouble with you, Sammy. It's celibacy."

"Perhaps," Sammy agreed. "If you've got a dictionary handy, I'll tell you."

"Get yourself a girl, Sammy," Leslie advised.

Sammy's brow clouded for a moment, and I knew he was thinking of a girl who must be dead now—but a girl he'd lost long before that. However, he rallied at once.

"You leaving Bill?" he asked. "I was wondering when you'd realize what a mistake you'd made. I'll think it over, Leslie. If I decide to accept your offer, I'll let you know."

Leslie merely grinned.

The Stowes, Caroline and John, were very self-sufficient. They did all that had to be done without complaining. They were always ready to help anyone who needed help, but they never asked for help themselves. Caroline, like Leslie and Betty, was pregnant, but unlike them, she didn't like anyone to mention it. Though she wasn't ashamed of the fact, it wasn't the sort of thing one talked about.

"She's still Miss Wallace, really," Leslie commented, without malice. "One of those women who can be a respectable matron and an old maid at the same time."

I grinned, because the remark was so just. Nevertheless I couldn't help saying: "Don't be rude about Caroline, Leslie. Did I ever tell you she came to me in Simsville and begged me to take you to Mars?"

"Did she?" asked Leslie, astonished. "I always thought she disapproved of me. Incidentally, did that influence you?"

"No," I said. "You and she were already on my list at the time."

Leslie started to say something, then stopped. That was something we still didn't talk about.

Jim Stowe was fourteen now, and with his first birthday on Mars he felt he was a man. He continued to be my personal assistant. His quick intelligence was soon known at all the stores and depots. I saw no reason to revise my idea that one day Jim would be a big man in the Martian settlement.

Harry Phillips was the same as ever, kindly and slow and phlegmatic. He couldn't smoke a pipe or drink a reflective half pint of beer any more, but that difficulty, which one might have thought would have taken half the savor out of life for him, didn't seem to bother him at all.

"Guess if I had a smoke now I'd wonder what I ever saw in tobacco," he said philosophically. "And I don't think I'd like the taste of beer any more. Been telling myself that, anyway. I've got more than halfway to believing it, too."

I tried several times to get Harry transferred to an agricultural unit, where he would be much more useful. However, the work party system was working so well that nobody wanted to break up any of the units if it could be helped. And Harry said that in the circumstances he'd just as soon stay with us.

I didn't see much of little Bessie these days. Young children were given jobs at the research station, making things, sorting things, running errands. It would be a long time yet before there was school again for the children. When there was, Leslie and Caroline would be back at their old jobs, teaching.

160

Anyway, I knew Bessie would be happy. She always was. That left only Betty and Morgan.

Betty put up a brave show. She always pretended she was perfectly happy and that Morgan and she got on very much as Leslie and I did, or the Stowes. We pretended to believe it.

Morgan continued to do only what he had to, sketchily, resentfully, without pride or interest in it. He couldn't be trusted to do anything on his own.

"Listen, Morgan," I said to him on one occasion. "Nobody's trying to make you do more than your fair share. I know you don't want to do this—think any of us do? Why we're doing it is so that we can all be comfortable again. We——"

"Shut up," said Morgan harshly. "I may have to work, but I don't have to listen to you."

"What's gone sour in you, Morgan?" I asked curiously. "Tell me—was I right to pick you for my lifeship crew, or did I make a mistake? Were you a cheap chiseler back on Earth too?"

That got under his skin. He flushed a dull red down to his shoulders. I was glad to see that, not because I wanted to get under his skin but because a man isn't hopeless so long as you can.

He didn't answer.

"What's eating you, Morgan?" I persisted.

"I'll tell you," he said suddenly, passionately. "I've heard you talk about human rights, but you still act the little dictator. You always have. We had to lick your boots back in Simsville—you had all the power, with nobody to check on you. On the lifeship you kept on being the big boss. Well, now I'm good and sick of you. I'm sick of being pushed around and worked like a slave and never being left alone. I didn't come here to be a slave. Who are you to talk about rights?"

I didn't remember talking about human rights, but I might have, and this was obviously one of Morgan's sore spots. I could tell that from the way he suddenly dragged the question of human rights from nowhere and got angry about it.

"Sometimes human rights have to be suspended for a bit," I said coolly. "Particularly such human rights as sitting on your backside and letting other people do the work."

Betty came along then. I tried to continue the discussion, but Morgan so obviously resented my bawling him out in front of Betty, as he considered it, that I shrugged and left them.

There was something in what he said about my being a dictator. I had to be. When things are grim, people have to be put in charge, people who say "Jump" and make sure everyone jumps without reporting in triplicate on their methods to some central bureau of justice.

The truth, I suspected, was not that Morgan was worried over the principle of the thing, as Sammy, say, might have been. Morgan didn't really mind someone giving the orders and cracking the whip to make sure they were immediately obeyed.

Morgan wanted to crack the whip himself.

I referred to the only law there was higher than the lieutenants—the council Sammy had told me about when I was still in the hospital. His description hadn't been unfair. Winant was governed by the original colony committee, plus the leaders who had emerged from the complements of the big spaceships, plus a few of the lieutenants themselves—never very many, not because we didn't all have the right to sit in on council meetings, but because there were seldom very many of us free to do so.

The council's advice on Morgan was merely: "Beat him. Starve him." It wasn't inhuman advice, it was inevitable. We were still fighting for our lives on Mars. Anyone among us who didn't pull his weight had to be kicked in the teeth until he did.

I tried docking Morgan's rations, without effect. Betty, I knew, was sharing hers with him, and I could hardly punish her too. I tried to make her see that Morgan must be brought into line, but as Leslie said: "That argument wouldn't have any effect on me, Bill, so why should it sway Betty?"

Sammy was surprised I didn't try the other suggestion. "I always thought you were a hard nut, Bill," he said. "But now when Morgan needs a swift kick in the pants, you won't give it to him."

I shrugged. "I'd beat anyone else, including you," I told him, "but I don't think it'll do Morgan the slightest good. He'll only resent it, hate me, hate everybody, and try to get even."

"He's doing that anyway," said Sammy, "so I don't see what harm it can do."

Morgan had taken up with an old acquaintance of mine, Alec Ritchie, who had just been discharged from the hospital with his leg in a cast. I remembered Ritchie showing interest in anyone who made a nuisance of himself.

"I never liked Ritchie," Sammy told Leslie and me. "Now that he and Morgan are hanging around together I know I was right."

I grinned. "Talk about bias," I said.

"No, I'm talking about Ritchie. Another thing. I don't like the way Morgan's been looking at Aileen Ritchie."

"Why, are you casting covetous eyes on Aileen?" demanded Leslie, interested.

"Just the words I was looking for," said Sammy. "Not that *I* am. Morgan is."

"Is what?"

"Casting covetous eyes on Aileen Ritchie."

"But he can't . . ." Suddenly Leslie realized that he could. Marriage didn't really count any more. Strictly, Betty and Morgan weren't married anyway. Neither were Leslie and I.

"Oh, Lord," I said, seeing more trouble.

"That would be the end of Betty," said Leslie vehemently. "She'd kill herself. I know it sounds crazy, but it's true. The poor kid still worships the ground Morgan treads on."

"I know," said Sammy. "That's why I don't like it."

"But Aileen wouldn't be such a fool . . ."

"Let's hope not," I said. "But frankly I don't see any happiness for Betty until Morgan does leave her. She certainly isn't happy with him."

We were uncomfortably silent after that. There was nothing anyone could do about Betty. Hers was one of those purely private tragedies which no one else can share or understand, and which most people prefer not to see.

I wondered what Ritchie could possibly want with Morgan.

4

Occasionally as the weeks passed I remembered Ritchie's words and wondered if there was anyone among the fugitives from Earth who was just waiting for a chance to step in and take over Winant. It was possible. It made too much sense.

The big, clumsy, badly constituted council was all that was needed while everyone was still working fourteen hours a day. Keep people busy enough and they don't need a government. They don't need much law either.

Eventually, however, the situation would change. And

what was being done to prepare for the time when we were no longer concerned merely with staying alive?

Nothing.

Nothing, at any rate, officially. Ritchie, of course, would be preparing. I didn't know anything of what his schemes would be, but I knew there would be schemes, all with the same object—the greatest possible power, success, comfort, safety, and freedom for Alec Ritchie.

And if there was one Alec Ritchie, there must be more. Possibly Ritchie himself would be a complete failure, his schemes collapsing about him in ruin. But some other smart Alec, some bigger and shrewder Ritchie, might even now be planning a future the council didn't dream of, yet a future that could swallow ours. Ritchie had put it plainly and neatly, and possibly even truly. I'd seen something of the sort happen on Earth, often.

The slow, patient, stupid peasant spends forty years saving enough to keep him in comfort for the rest of his life. And the smart, smooth, practiced con man spends forty minutes taking it away from him.

The small child slowly gathers a fine collection of shells. The bigger child acquires the whole collection by the simple method of taking it from him.

It's not as easy to take over a community like Winant as it is to take shells from a small child. Of course not. But does the peasant expect to lose his money? Does the child expect to lose his shells? No, and we were putting ourselves in line by not expecting anyone to become a dictator in Winant.

At that point I usually laughed at myself and thought of some more pleasant aspect of the future, like whether we were going to have a son or a daughter, and what we were going to call him or her.

There was no money in the settlement, and a lot of people, myself included, thought we could get on very nicely without it. When the so-called labor units came in, however, we lieutenants had to take notice of them. There were different kinds of labor units at first. The root idea behind them all was that people who wanted something made promises of one kind or another, the prospective seller insisted on having them in writing, and the buyer drew up a contract and signed it.

And before we knew it we had money again.

The principal thing that could replace money, of course, was service. People would promise, in return for something, that when they were able they would do some job or other. Sometimes the promise was to replace the article at some future date with another of slightly better quality. These promises were written down and became, inevitably, negotiable.

When we realized we had to do something about this innovation we were already too late to catch the first profiteers of the new settlement. Some cunning characters had been quick to realize the possibility of gain in this system. With their uncanny instinct for profit they had sold all they had to sell, plus a lot that they didn't, exchanged the tokens they gained for others, gave out promises of their own, shuffled their gains about with the magical sleight of hand of the brilliant businessman, sold them to the right people at the right moment, bought back their own promises, and generally kept things on the move, with each move meaning a little more in their own pockets. It was they who flooded the market with bad currency—promises that could never be fulfilled, made by people who would promise anything— while the real, hard cash, the tokens of the people who kept their word, was in their pockets.

We saw we couldn't stop this practice, we could only check it, standardize and administer it. We'd have liked to cancel all previous transactions, but we couldn't.

Lieutenants became bankers along with all the other things they had to do. Came the one-labor unit, representing certain stated service, the five-labor unit and the ten. We forbade anything above the ten, at first. Labor unit became labit, then laby. We had abandoned dollars, francs, pounds, marks, pesos, lire, rupees, kronen, rubles, and acquired, to replace them all, the laby. Every laby had to represent a genuine promise of service, and was countersigned by a lieutenant. It wasn't long before we were using watermarked paper, and money was back.

Close on the heels of this came another new factor connected with it.

Morgan didn't appear to work one day on the building we were erecting, but someone, a Czechoslovakian who spoke very little English, came in his place. On investigating I found he'd been paid to do Morgan's job. He was satisfied; he was a tough, honest fellow who could do two men's work. One man's work he had to do for nothing, but he could get money for the extra work he did. He must somehow have arranged his freedom from his own party, by doing three days' work in two, perhaps.

I couldn't do a thing. I didn't know where Morgan got the money—he wasn't the kind of smart businessman who could take advantage of any opportunity to line his pockets—but I could guess. Alec Ritchie, I was certain, *was* the kind of smart businessman who could take advantage of any opportunity to line his pockets, and had.

That day was notable for more than the reintroduction of paid service.

Group 94 was being transferred to the excavations, now well advanced, and three of us went on ahead to see what we were going to have to do, while the rest, minus Morgan and plus his hired hand, carried on at the old job under Sammy. The three who went were Leslie, Betty, and I.

Betty seemed unnaturally gay. She wasn't a talker as a rule, but on this occasion she talked so much that Leslie and I could hardly get a word in. I caught Leslie's inquiring glance once or twice, and wondered whether to ask Betty bluntly what the matter was. It would be something to do with Morgan, of course.

However, Leslie suddenly asked, when Betty stopped talking for a moment: "Are you feeling all right, Betty?"

Leslie must have seen things I missed. I hadn't noticed anything physically wrong with Betty. But I knew Leslie was on the right track when Betty said swiftly:

"No, it's just the air pressure. I'm all right."

Human beings always have to have a handy excuse for everything, and on Mars the reduced air pressure was blamed for a lot of things it didn't do. Mars really had a very thick envelope of air, much thicker than anyone had thought before the first ship reached Mars. The only thing Mars couldn't do in this respect was make the air weigh so much. Mars had a surprisingly high air pressure, but it was well short of what we were used to.

Knowing this, people used it as an excuse for being tired, or stiff, or having a headache, or not wanting to work, or whatever it was they wanted an excuse for. But in actual fact it had scarcely any perceptible effect on us at all, beyond reducing the boiling point of water so that what we called hot water ceased to exist except in a laboratory. Or rather, it had the same effect on all of us. We adapted to it, as we adapted to the reduced gravity. We couldn't help it.

So when Betty made the new but already old excuse I knew she was hiding something.

"You don't feel sick, do you?" I asked.

"No, it's nothing. Forget it."

Obviously it made her feel worse when we talked about it. I noticed now that she was a little unsteady on her feet. Since she wanted to talk about something else, anything else, we let her do it.

About two minutes later she reeled in a sudden gust of wind. I caught her, quite gently, and steadied her. But at my touch she stiffened and collapsed in a faint.

"Leslie," I said, "have a look at her. She fainted when I put my arm around her."

I paced about as Leslie bent over the girl. I was hoping fervently that this was nothing over which I would have to take action. I was quite sure that what I'd told Sammy about Morgan was right. The only hope for Morgan was that bit

169

by bit he could be made to realize clearly and plainly what he was doing and see just how that conduct fitted, or didn't fit, in the fabric of the fight for existence of a tiny remnant of all the peoples of Earth.

I heard Leslie catch her breath sharply and knew that ignoring this wasn't going to be possible.

"I think you'd better have a look at her, Bill," said Leslie. There was fury in her voice which I had never heard before.

There was no sign of Betty's pregnancy yet. Her belly was thin and flat, and it was one big angry bruise. There was hardly a square inch of clear, undamaged skin below the waist. It was no surprise at all that Betty had fainted at a touch. How she could have come by those injuries I found it difficult to guess. I didn't think merely pounding her with a fist could have done that.

Leslie was too angry to speak. I wasn't angry, after one wild surge of rage, just tired, disappointed, and sorry. The man who could do that could do anything. He could easily have killed Betty; the fact that she was able to walk about and pretend nothing had happened to her wasn't his fault.

"Now I'll have to beat him," I said wearily, "and if we don't watch them day and night he'll take it out of Betty. Until finally he kills her. Then we can shoot or hang Morgan, and the air around here will be a little cleaner."

"He's not going to kill Betty!" exclaimed Leslie fiercely.

"I don't see how we can stop him," I said. "She won't leave him, even now. We can't execute him, or put him in prison, or extradite him. All we can do is wait till he kills someone, and then by ordinary, common-sense law we can execute him to stop him from killing anyone else."

I went on in weary bitterness: "God, to think I did this. I could have done better by picking the first lounger I saw in the street——"

Betty stirred and opened her eyes. She looked up at us, searched our faces, and then suddenly felt the breeze on her skin. With a convulsive movement she sat up, wincing, and grabbed her suit.

170

"Let me do it," said Leslie. She eased the garment carefully over the bruised flesh.

"I fell," said Betty quickly. "It was during the gale yesterday——"

"Hell, you're not going to cover up for Morgan now, are you?" I demanded.

"It wasn't Morgan. It was——"

"How did he do it?" I asked.

She capitulated. She burst into tears, crying as I had never seen a woman cry before. She didn't weep with passion, but with grief and misery and hopelessness.

Through her tears, in choked phrases, she told us what had happened.

Morgan had taken her far out in the desert the night before, just after sunset. He had told her she mustn't have her baby. If she did, he would kill it. She had been crying, begging, screaming, but he slapped her face until she was quiet. He asked her if she knew how to arrange a miscarriage. She didn't. It hadn't occurred to her that any woman had ever tried to arrange a miscarriage. Even slapping her face couldn't stop her crying and pleading again.

He threw her down and started hitting her with a round stone, sitting on her chest to hold her down. Betty didn't know how long that went on. She thought she had been unconscious for a while, but when she revived he was still beating her with the stone. Finally he said, "That ought to do it," threw the stone away, and let her get up, when she could.

"But *why*, Betty?" said Leslie wonderingly. "Did he say why?"

Through a fresh flood of tears Betty said: "He said he's going to have Aileen Ritchie. He said he didn't want me and a kid I could say was his always hanging around his neck. Now I'll lose my baby and——"

"You won't," I said. "Not if you keep away from Morgan in future and don't give him another chance."

The tears stopped abruptly. "I won't lose my baby?" Betty asked incredulously.

"I don't think so. Morgan doesn't know a thing about it, which is just as well. Keep clear of him and you'll have your baby all right."

"But I can't keep clear of him! I love him."

I knew that. I'd thought about it already. I sighed. "Make sure he never has a chance to do anything like that again, then."

Betty looked almost happy. "Then we can forget all about it?" she asked hopefully.

Leslie's eyes met mine. "No, Betty," I said sadly. "We can never forget all about it. A man can beat his wife or throw her about a bit and it's nobody's business but their own. But when a man does what Morgan's done to you, it's everybody's business."

"Please," Betty pleaded. "Let Morgan and me——"

"No, Betty," I repeated patiently. "Do you want Morgan to kill you and your baby?"

When Morgan appeared that evening I waited until his paid deputy had gone, and then drew the whole group together in the husk of the building we were helping to erect. I wasn't dramatic. I told them simply what was going to happen and precisely why. Morgan went ashen and tried to run for it, but Sammy was right behind him.

I made Betty show them all what Morgan had done to her. I had to do that, because Betty was quite capable of denying, at some future date, that Morgan had ever assaulted her at all. At the gasps and cries and murmurs of anger that were loosed I surveyed Morgan to see if there was any sign of regret. There was none—only fear of what was going to happen to him.

Well, fear it would have to be, then. He would have to leave Betty alone because he was afraid to touch her, if that was the only restraint that could be put on him.

I didn't ask them to stay while I whipped Morgan. The only purpose in public punishment is to deter others, and the others didn't need deterring. Sammy stayed, that was all. I got Leslie to take Betty away.

Sammy had said he always thought I was a hard nut. When I whipped Morgan I discovered quite definitely that I wasn't. Each time he screamed, and he screamed often, the sound crawled in my guts. I couldn't see what pleasure anyone could get in hurting other people. It made me sick.

I had to keep reminding myself, as I'd told Morgan again and again, that this wasn't punishment for the past, it was warning for the future. Any time he wanted to act like a beast in the future, I told him over and over again, he would have to decide whether it was worth being beaten half to death afterward.

When it was over Morgan was moaning and crying together. I didn't blame him for that. I'd given him just about all he could take.

And once again I tried to drive the lesson home. "The next time, Morgan," I said quietly, "it will be worse."

Sammy and I left him. I wouldn't meet Sammy's eyes. I still felt it had had to be done, but I wasn't proud of having done it.

"If you'd carried on just a little longer," Sammy said, "you might have left him feeling so low that he'd have killed himself."

I stared at him in surprise.

"It would be much better that way," said Sammy moodily. "Morgan's never going to be any use to anybody."

I thought of that as an epitaph, and shuddered.

MORGAN SMITH
He was never any use to anybody.

For once, all the lieutenants were called together to vote on some of the big questions. It was time we had a properly constituted government. There was no question of that.

It was some meeting. There were nearly two thousand present, in the biggest hall at the research station and in dozens of other rooms around it, hearing what was going on by a big public-address link-up. Every room had to have a sort of chairman to keep his group in order and not have the P.A. system choked with babble.

One of the things we did was vote ourselves out of power, as lieutenants. Some of us were pretty fed up with the job anyway. We had a little power and a lot of extra work. Others knew that though they might have been the right men to command lifeships, they weren't the right men for the job they had now. We agreed that the groups of eleven, the lifeship crews, should stay units for the moment, but each should elect its own leader. Representatives would also be returned in the same way by the big ships' complements and by the members of the original colony.

There was a long discussion about whether it was a good thing to keep representation in three groups like that. Somebody said we should have government for the whole population, not representatives who stood for the special interests of different groups. But it was agreed in the end that there were no special interests. It no longer mattered whether people had been on Mars all along or had come in the big ships or in the lifeships.

We were building a new council from scratch, at last, instead of trying to patch up some existing organization. Nobody imagined it would be perfect. It would be better, that was all. The next council, we hoped, would be better still.

We might have gone back and held our elections right away, so that it would be the new council who settled the other problems we had before us. However, on another vote we decided that, rather than throw the new council in at the deep end, we'd give them something to work on and amend. We'd make the decisions and go on giving the orders for a week longer before throwing the council open to everybody. We had some experience of command, after all. The new members would have to learn how to apply it.

We agreed that the laby system was out of our control. We could avoid what might be called inflation and deflation, that was all.

Marriage was abolished temporarily. There had been a lot

174

of trouble over that, people wanting someone to marry them, people wanting someone to give them divorces, people living together without marriage, people formally married sneering at people informally married and saying they were living in sin. It seemed that the best answer was not to elevate formal marriage and give away or refuse divorces, but at one bold stroke to destroy immorality and leave sex relations to—of all things—common sense.

Then there was another long discussion on the problem of language, race, and nation.

Our twenty thousand plus was composed of white men, black men, brown men, and yellow men, speaking English, French, Chinese, Russian, German, Italian, Arabic, Swahili, and scores of other languages. Agreement on English as the standard language was surprisingly easy, but agreement that the other languages should die was as difficult as anyone would have expected.

You couldn't blame the Spaniards, with their Cervantes, the Greeks, with their glorious classical age, the Germans, with their Goethe and Schiller and Heine, for objecting. I don't have to put their case, it's so obvious. However, the case for English as not merely the standard language but the *only* language was pretty good too. Without language barriers we'd have a much better chance of real unity than Earth ever had.

We didn't settle that question. It was clear we couldn't, just then. But it would probably work itself out. If people had to speak English to be understood, the other languages would die, year by year, generation by generation.

Again, it was with surprisingly little trouble that we agreed that mating between any female and any male should be permitted, outside the blood relationships which would exist again in the next generation. Some of the Americans, Germans, and Africans were violently against miscegenation. The French didn't give a damn. The South Africans and Australians wouldn't even talk about it. The English thought it would be a good thing, in theory.

175

And it was in theory that we agreed on it. We couldn't solve a problem like that merely by voting on it. But the vote meant that we hoped the Martian colony would one day comprise one people and one race, speaking one language.

It all sounded very fine.

We decided to go on as at present with soil preparation and building as the two over-all priorities. We formed a banking unit to supervise laby transactions, a medical unit to check on a few new (fortunately mild) illnesses that were appearing in the new conditions, and an exploration unit to survey Mars, chiefly for rich soil.

5

Came the day of the great storm, which modified most of our plans.

It started like any ordinary gale. I was out alone, about half a mile from the research station, looking for another vein of the red rock we'd been using. When the wind started I dropped flat. Usually the winds didn't last. You waited for a calm period and then made for shelter.

The first indication I had that this wasn't an ordinary wind was when I was lifted like a feather, whirled in the air, swept along about twenty yards, and then dashed to the ground. I was lucky in being dropped on one of the thickest patches of lichen. I was only jarred from tip to toe. No bones were broken.

Presently I wasn't so sure that I had been lucky in my landing ground. The lichen offered no purchase at all. At least the rocks were something to hang onto. Another gust came and I was lifted again. I spun crazily, touched the ground with one foot, somersaulted, and bounced off the lichen again. I was bowled along, half lifted, half rolled, for fully a hundred yards. This time, however, I came to a stop against a spur of rock to which I clung grimly.

The gale, insofar as it had direction, was coming from Winant. Fairly safe for the moment, I looked to see what was being blown from there—and there was plenty. There were sheets of metal, tarpaulins, doors, bits of masonry—and people, little black, struggling things whirling like confetti from an electric fan. I was thankful that my group was working in the vast hole in front of the station. They would be safe, if anyone was.

A naked body shot past me, twenty feet in the air. I knew the man was dead, because his head was flapping from side to side like a flag. He still wore his shoes, but his suit had been torn off him. Fifty yards to the right a woman was swept past. She was still alive—she saw me and made a wild gesture of appeal. I could do nothing, of course. The only hope anyone had in a storm like that was to find an anchor, as I had done, and stay put.

Just for an instant, and then it was gone, I heard a distant crash. I scanned Winant, my eyes stung by the wind, streaming with tears. The gale had actually lifted a lifeship and cast it down again across half a dozen others. As I looked, another lifeship was torn loose and spun crazily along across the plain.

I wondered if this was going to be the end of it all for Winant and for the people from Earth. My arms were aching; an extra-strong gust and I should be swept away again. No one else could be in much better state except the people in the pit, and those in the station itself. Even if the storm stopped at once, the toll must be enormous.

The fate of the community was going to depend very largely on the number of people who happened to be in the pit and the station at the time. I had no up-to-date information on who was working where. If there had been only a thousand actually at the station and fifty in the pit—which was possible—Winant might drop in one day below the critical level for survival.

As if to show that even the people in the pit weren't safe, the wind suddenly threw up a vast black cloud of dust which completely obscured Winant. Hundreds of tons of dust and sand must be showering into the excavations.

I was trying not to see the things and people flying past me. Winant I could do nothing about, but it seemed that I should at least try to help the poor wretches who were blown past, helpless, most of them dead but some all too obviously still alive. I felt guilty because I was safe.

In a black shower, what seemed like half Winant hurled across the plain two hundred yards away. There were cattle, helpless in the gale; men and women, clawing wildly at the air, desperately seeking something to hang on to; loose stones, clothing, and thousands of small objects I couldn't identify. As I watched, unable to look away, the whole dark cloud was dashed to the ground, disintegrated like a bombed house, and swept on in a dozen streamlets.

I saw one man grasp a rock as I had done. He took a firm hold with both arms. Just for an instant relief must have flooded him. Then a big, dark object that might have been part of a wall struck him in the back with such force that it broke the rock through him, and all together they swept on before the gale—masonry, broken rock, and indeterminate pieces of animal tissue.

A youth whose mind must have given way flew past gracefully, flapping his arms like a bird's wings and laughing in ecstasy. I watched him into the distance, still beating his arms as if he had discovered the secret of flight.

Far out to my right I saw a speck high in the air, higher than any debris I had seen so far. It had thin, waving tendrils that must be arms and legs. Abruptly it fell as the wind, which had supported it, died for an instant. I saw it plummet down almost to the ground. Then it was swept away again, only a few feet above the plain, as if the gale was playing with it.

When I looked back toward Winant I saw three people quite near me rolling in line across the plain, like a grotesque act in an acrobatic show. I started when I saw the middle one clearly for an instant. It was Aileen Ritchie. Dust blinded me for long seconds. When I could see again, two of the three were gone, but Aileen was clinging to the same spur of rock as I was, forty yards away. As I saw her, she nearly lost her grip. She seemed to be hurt, which was no surprise at all.

I had been able to ignore the people I didn't know, treating them as puppets in the wild, mad scene, no more aidable than the shadows on a movie screen. But crazy though it might be to move from my comparatively safe anchorage, I had to try to help someone I did know. I started clawing my way along the ridge to Aileen.

In two places the ridge was broken, the wind whistling through the gap. I'd have stopped at the first if it hadn't been obvious that, left unaided, Aileen was going to be swept away in a few minutes. I don't know quite how I did cross the two gaps. I certainly didn't walk, and I didn't crawl. I must simply have thrown myself across and grabbed the rock.

Just before I reached Aileen the thought crossed my mind that if it had been Morgan, not she, a problem would have been solved. I could have stayed put and watched him fight his battle with the storm and lose it. But I couldn't be sure that I'd have let even Morgan die. In a turmoil like that, a man might be insane enough to risk his life to save an enemy, simply to try to cheat the gale and because they were both human beings.

I reached Aileen and grasped her firmly. I had seen her

180

often and nodded to her, but I had never actually spoken to her except for those few words in the hospital.

"Thanks," she gasped. "I couldn't have lasted much longer."

"Let's get five yards back," I said. I could feel the words being ripped out of my mouth and swept away across the desert. "There's a safe place for both of us."

We made it with a struggle. The ridge was only about four feet high, but at that point there was a crack into which we could wedge ourselves. We jammed our legs in together and stood breast to breast like dancers in a ballroom. Aileen could lean back a little against the rock, and did. She seemed rather embarrassed. The situation was too serious for me to be embarrassed at all.

"Where are you hurt?" I asked.

"Arm, side, and head, I think," she said.

I checked her injuries, but they seemed minor—minor, at any rate, while the world was being blown apart at the seams. She wasn't going to be able to use her left arm for a day or two, her fair hair was clotted with blood, and she had a six-inch gash in her side—but what was that when hundreds of people were being dashed to pulp all about us?

"What happened to the rest of 92?" I asked.

"They're all right. They got under cover. I didn't quite make it. How about your group, Lieutenant Easson?"

"In the pit," I said. I grinned wryly. "In the circumstances, Aileen, I think you might call me Bill."

She smiled. "I suppose so, Bill. How long do you think this'll last?"

"Since nothing quite like this has happened before, any guesses I might make would be worthless. I'd have thought it would have been over long since."

Instead of its being over, we suddenly found ourselves enveloped in the dust cloud of all time. We shut our eyes, not only to protect them, but because we couldn't see anything anyway.

The flying dust and sand pierced our skin like thousands

of tiny needles. I felt a sharp twinge in my neck as a cloud of sand peppered it like buckshot. I put my hand to the back of my neck and it came away sticky with blood.

Then just as the worst of the dust storm seemed to be over and I opened my eyes cautiously, rain swept over us, hammering our skin, beating on our temples.

Aileen's voice came to me from a long way off. "You don't mind if I . . . ?" She straightened against me and put her arms around me.

I clutched her tightly. "I don't mind at all," I said.

In a few seconds we were awash, water running down from our shoulders to our ankles. I felt a stream from Aileen's knee transferring itself to my calf. Gradually the gray dust that had covered us was washed away, like chalk marks on a wall when a shower starts.

Aileen was crying. Her tears seemed to surprise her more than they surprised me. She made a desperate effort to stop, and told me fiercely: "I don't know why I'm doing this. It's not because I'm hurt."

I understood, because I felt like crying too. I've heard of men doing it in storms on Earth, when their utter impotence is brought home to them. Here there was all there had been in storms on Earth, plus the insecurity and helplessness of being so lightly secured to the surface of the world by the weak, tenuous gravity.

The rain lasted only two minutes or so. Then the character of the wind changed. It began to come in sudden, incredibly fierce gusts, followed by comparative calm.

Aileen mastered herself at last. She cast a quick, ashamed glance up at my face, still clinging to me.

"Think nothing of it," I said. "It's enough to make anyone cry."

"I feel such a baby," she said vehemently. "So weak and useless—if you weren't here I wouldn't last five minutes in this."

Out of the fog of dust which was still streaming overhead a huge, gleaming shape dropped abruptly. We couldn't move.

182

We waited to be crushed to death, hugging each other convulsively.

However, its size had deceived us. It crashed down fully fifty yards away, broke in two, and was swept away on the wings of the wind again. We didn't hear the sound of the crash at all. It was entirely dissipated by the storm.

"What was that?" asked Aileen.

"Lifeship," I said. I was thinking of how that ship had come safely from Earth to Mars, and had then been destroyed by a mere wind.

Suddenly the wind died. We were left feeling rather foolish, clinging tightly to each other as protection against a storm that no longer existed.

"Can that be the end?" Aileen whispered. It seemed natural to whisper in the sudden silence.

"Probably, but while we're here we're safe. Let's wait until the dust settles a little. I'll have a look at that gash of yours, now that there's water to——"

"I'd rather you didn't," said Aileen quickly.

"As you like," I said equably.

"I'm sorry, I only meant——"

I grinned. "I know." I prised myself out and sat on the rock. Aileen pulled herself up beside me.

"Bill, I should have known better," she said humbly. "*Please* see if you can do anything about that gash."

"Stop apologizing, Aileen." I smiled. "And don't make an issue of it. I don't think you thought I thought whatever it was. Come on, I'll carry you to the hospital."

"I can walk."

"Perhaps, but it isn't necessary. You realize that if I carry you I'm still only moving point six nine of what I used to have to tote around all the time on Earth?"

She chuckled. "That's so. All right, go ahead."

We lost our lightness of manner before we'd gone far. The ground was strewn with debris, human and otherwise. And a glance showed that the crops some of us had labored over were all destroyed.

"We can't say Mars gave us no warning," I said heavily. "There were light winds and strong winds. We should have been ready for an occasional much stronger wind."

I left her at the research station and went to the pit, refusing to look about me and see how much of our work was ruined.

The great storm killed 2590 people and injured 6000 more. It put us back where we had started as far as food was concerned, and killed so many cattle that the remainder would have to be watched and tended and bred very carefully if the species were not to die out. It showed that only buildings as strong as the research station itself were of any use on the surface of Mars. It put an end once and for all to all grumbles and complaints about working on permanent buildings. It demonstrated clearly to anyone and everyone how shaky our foothold on Mars still was, and how risky it was to relax until we had made it a lot more secure. It undermined the new laby system, since so many contracts which had been perfectly good the day before were now worthless.

In many ways the results of the gale were good. But no one would have wanted these things at such a cost. Besides, in one or two not so immediately obvious ways the results of the storm were not good.

One big change in plan was inevitable. Before this the general construction plan had been to construct fair-sized buildings around the research station and use the pit, the cave homes, more or less for temporary housing. The ground-level building was the important thing and the below-ground-level work stopgap and experimental.

After the storm the plan was reversed. Flats carved in solid rock, reinforced by concrete and steel, and below ground level, were obviously much safer than buildings on the surface which, as had just been demonstrated, were very vulnerable while they were in course of construction. We would make a huge square a hundred feet deep, and build on only two sides. Later we could make it even bigger, and finally we should have a warm, sheltered garden all over the floor of the square, with comfortable, solid flats all around.

True, at first the flats would be makeshift. But that way we could develop in safety. By building on the surface we should always be at the mercy of a great storm like that first one.

Group 94 came through the storm unharmed. Once I knew that, I could help to assess the damage it had done with more equanimity.

Aileen wasn't seriously hurt. She was at the hospital only a few minutes. There were too many people more seriously hurt for the hospital staff to pay much attention to mere gashes and lumps on the head.

She came and tried to thank me for saving her life. Leslie interrupted her. "He enjoyed it, Aileen," she said. "Now he'll save your life any time he gets a chance, and kiss you again."

"He didn't kiss me!" Aileen protested.

"Why not?" Leslie asked me, puzzled.

"I don't like blondes," I told her.

6

When the first informal election was held, I was voted PL. The word "lieutenant" had never been a very good description—we had been called lieutenants merely to give us some sort of pseudo-military authority over the people back on Earth whom we were taking, or not taking, to Mars. We now became known as party leaders. But since that phrase had political connotations we didn't like, the initials were generally used.

There was no opposition to my election as PL, not even from Morgan. Morgan had been quieter, rather to my surprise, since I whipped him. He never did anything to suggest that he regretted what he had done to Betty; in fact, there was all too little doubt that he was one of those compulsive sadists who could no more keep his hands off his girl than an addict could stop taking drugs. He and Betty still fought like wildcats, and of course Betty invariably came off worst. But there was never anything for which I could whip Morgan again. He always stopped short of doing her any real harm.

She would have a bruise on her face, and say it was nothing. Or there would be blue marks on her thin wrists. Once when she turned up with her arm and shoulder bandaged, I was going to go for Morgan again, whatever Betty said. But it transpired that this time he really had had nothing to do with it. She had been dashed against a wall by the winds.

The suspension of marriage didn't do their relations any good. Morgan didn't say outright that he was finished with Betty, but he made it clear that he didn't mind whether she stayed with him or not. Betty, poor kid, still loved the man.

I had guessed for some time that Ritchie was one of the leading profiteers, and that Morgan was tied up with him in some way. After the storm there was no pretense at all. Ritchie had done very well out of the storm, and didn't mind admitting it.

With so many people dying, the whole laby system had taken a knock, since a lot of the contracts in circulation were suddenly valueless. Ritchie apparently followed out the time-hallowed process of forcing the market as low as it would go, buying all he could and then letting the market rise again. I didn't follow any of his transactions in detail, but the general line was obvious.

"You're a reasonable fellow, Bill," he told me good-humoredly when I met him once. "You must know that when anything happens—anything at all—there's always something for a smart man to make out of it. Now I'll repeat an offer I made once before. If you'd like to come in with me——"

"Ritchie," I said grimly, "you're a reasonable fellow too, in your own way, and you know damn well before you say any more that I'm not going to come in with you in any of your schemes."

Ritchie laughed as if I had made a very good joke. "That's what I like about you, Bill," he said warmly. "Cards always on the table, and no dealing off the bottom of the deck. Well, I'll be just as frank with you. From what I hear you saved Aileen's life, and I never like to feel I owe any man anything. So——"

"So you offer me a chance you know I'm not going to take?"

"Yes," said Ritchie blandly. "You see, *I* think I'm making you a very good offer—or I would, if you'd let me. If *you* don't like it, and turn it down, that's not my fault, is it?"

I couldn't help laughing at the insolence of this cheerful rogue.

"Call it quits, Ritchie," I said. "I like Aileen, despite the fact that she's your daughter. I'll save her life any time. How did she come to be your daughter, anyway?"

"She takes after her mother," Ritchie admitted.

You could say things like that to Ritchie. It wasn't possible to insult him. Not only did he never seem to bear malice, he never did bear malice. And yet nobody liked him. People are hard to please, aren't they?

Sometimes he reminded me of a bland, attentive *maître d'hôtel* who had far more money than the people he served so gracefully and assiduously. His manner must have helped him a lot. He would always, I imagined, give the impression of wanting to lend you money, wanting to help you. And only afterward would you realize how much helping you had helped him.

Sometimes, too, he reminded me of the beautiful, experienced women who have really learned the art of being escorted. Women like that let you take them out, pay enormous sums for their entertainment, wine, and dinner, take them home, kiss their hands, and leave you with the impression that it's been a wonderful privilege.

188

I kept finding and hearing of more and more people who in some way, to some limited extent, were in Ritchie's hands. Money was becoming, once more, a necessity, and Ritchie had money.

There were the work schemes, for example. Ritchie, still unable to work himself because of his broken leg, bought and sold labor, and nobody could do a thing about it. It was known that if you wanted a day off Ritchie could arrange it. Four or five other people would work for you, by Ritchie's arrangement, and you would sign what amounted to labies for your day's work, plus something. Even if the something was very small, there was no telling how little replacing you had actually cost Ritchie. The men who filled in for you might be heavy debtors to Ritchie, doing the job to escape a little interest.

Of course it was crazy for anyone to agree to such a thing. Most of the people who did so knew that. This was how it came about that anyone ever did.

You get into a fitful sleep at last about two hours before dawn. You are wakened with everyone else, lightheaded and gummy-eyed, stiff and sore, and you know you have a hard, heavy day's work in front of you. You think of going to the doctor, but unless you are genuinely ill that won't do you any good. You know there is a way you can have a day of glorious freedom, freedom to lie in bed if you like, go around and watch everyone else work if you like, go out and walk in the desert if you like. You shake your head and go out and work.

The next day the same temptation is before you. And every day, until at last you allow yourself just one day off. Ritchie arranges it, and it is glorious. All day you have no regrets. You are quite decided that as soon as possible you will redeem your labies . . . somehow.

That's how it happened. Ritchie was given a great chance by the inflexibility of our rules. They had to be inflexible. We couldn't allow people to do what they liked, when they liked, because there was far too much to be done. It had to be an all-out, enforced effort by everybody. Particularly after the storm had shown how acute and how immediate the problem of food and shelter was.

When the new council of PLs was elected, it met at once to decide a few more things which now had to be decided.

We passed a law that no one should be able to control more than a certain amount of laby cash at any one time. It wasn't a good law, and right away we had to make an exception in favor of the party leaders, the council members. Promptly Alec Ritchie was returned by his section as a PL.

The truth of the matter was that if there was to be law at all there was no way of stopping the rise to power of people like Ritchie. The law is always blind; it protects the honest and the dishonest, the rich and poor, the good and evil, the intelligent and the stupid. And since it's better understood and better applied by the intelligent, the evil, the rich and dishonest people, it always protects them far more than anyone else.

Morgan, with Ritchie's approval, wanted Aileen. But Aileen very clearly didn't want Morgan. She kept him at arm's length, and Ritchie didn't interfere.

The Ritchie situation had been inevitable. For the most part the people who had been brought to Mars were as intelligent and co-operative and good-natured as we could have hoped. The choice, however, couldn't be perfect; people like Ritchie and Morgan slipped through.

We accomplished a tremendous amount in a few months following the storm. When men and women realize that what they're doing is for their own personal safety, the job is liable to be done quickly and well.

Leslie's arm was completely healed. Like so many women in the settlement, she was doing her last spell of hard work before easing off in the late stages of pregnancy. Leslie was one of those rare women who could continue to be attractive right through pregnancy. Wanting the baby was part of it. Not being unduly concerned about her appearance helped too. But most of the reason was probably that Leslie was attractive independent of being beautiful. She would have been attractive if she had been fat or had gap teeth.

Twenty thousand is a pretty big labor force, particularly when things are so easy to carry that cranes and trucks are virtually unnecessary. When a force like that is really working together it can accomplish wonders.

We dug out our cliff and our caves and moved in. At first there were twenty-five so-called flats in a row and eight levels. Then we dug out a similar block at right angles. For the first time since we left Earth a few lucky couples had something resembling a bedroom to themselves. And of course every time someone moved into a flat conditions at the research station became slightly better.

People are delighted at even a small improvement in their living conditions if there has been no improvement at all for a long time. If they had been sleeping ten in a room, they found it sheer luxury when two went away and there were only eight left.

We seemed to have turned the corner merely because every month things were better. But there was no serious slacking off. It might be very nice to be sharing a room at the research station with only seven other people, but it would naturally be better still if there were only six in the room.

Leslie and I had a room to ourselves. It wasn't finished; in fact, by some standards it would have been said to be barely started. It was a little bubble drilled out of the rock. It would eventually be the kitchen of the three-room flat we were at present sharing with two other couples. But we had no complaints; not after months of sleeping in a tiny room at the research station with four other couples.

The four hundred flats begun so far thus took about twenty-five hundred people. The one big building completed on the surface, already known as the barracks, accommodated seven hundred. A warren of purely temporary caves, corridors, galleries, and cubicles blasted and hewn in one of the cliff faces, which would eventually be cleared away, gave shelter to twelve hundred single men and was thus called bachelors' hall. A similar temporary warren on the fourth side of the pit accommodated eight hundred single women, and was called old maids' hostel, though not generally by the inmates themselves, who had other ideas. The lifeships behind the research station still housed about two thousand, and the other spaceships a further thousand. All that came to eighty-two hundred, leaving not much over ten thousand to be housed at the research station. And since it had been built for seven thousand people, we weren't too badly off all around.

A day came when we had another storm, not quite so fierce as the great storm, but out of the same stable, and no one was killed. About fifty people were injured. That was all the storm could do. It didn't put work back at all.

There was general rejoicing. In a few months more we could be ready for another great storm. We should be able to snap our fingers at it.

Suddenly most of the women were having babies. They all dated from about the same time—the moment, on the lifeships, when it must have been clear to the lieutenants in charge how little chance there was of landing safely on Mars. It wasn't clear whether these children had been conceived in wild, unreasonable hope or in complete despair.

Aileen Ritchie came to see us one evening after work.

"Hello," said Leslie, rather surprised. "You want to see Bill about something?"

"No," said Aileen. "I trained as a nurse once. I wondered if you could use some help?"

"Thanks," said Leslie warmly. "Caroline's supposed to be looking after Betty and me, but it won't be long before she has her baby too. We'll be glad of your help."

All sorts of arrangements had been made to deal with the situation. However, no matter how efficient the arrangements were, there were too many women having babies at once for the comparatively few doctors, nurses, and midwives to deal with them all. The strong, healthy girls like Leslie would have to have their babies with such half-qualified assistance as they could get. Betty was another matter. She was already at the hospital under the doctors' eyes. Betty's labor wasn't going to be easy at best. She was too thin and frail and narrow-hipped.

I had had no particular worries about Leslie, largely because she obviously wasn't worried herself. I was glad to see Aileen coming to help, all the same.

We talked for a long time. Aileen and Leslie had long ago formed one of those casual feminine acquaintanceships which always puzzle men. They didn't seek each other out, and Leslie never mentioned Aileen, yet when they happened to be together there was no restraint between them and any male in their company was apt to feel neglected. They were alike, they understood one another, they didn't have to explain things, and they were friendly without being wildly enthusiastic about each other. Aileen and Leslie acted rather like some sisters-in-law I had known who got on well together but didn't see each other much.

They certainly had one of those mysterious feminine alliances which exclude all males and quite a few females. Half the time when they were talking I didn't know what was going on. It's good for a man to see his wife as a partner in such an alliance now and then—keeps him from coming to the dangerous conclusion that he knows all there is to be known about her.

Another thing is that men together and women together have different standards of what they tell each other and what they don't. There are things men don't tell men and things women don't tell women, but they don't coincide. I was startled at some of the things Aileen and Leslie casually told each other, and puzzled when, obviously by mutual agreement, they avoided things that men would have made no bones about discussing.

I left them after a bit and looked in on Sammy at bachelors' hall. I told him about Aileen, of course. I always tried to mention Aileen in a favorable light to Sammy, which was easy enough because I had never heard or seen anything against her except that Alec Ritchie was her father. I had no real intention of playing matchmaker, but I could see no reason why Sammy and Aileen shouldn't get together.

Sammy had been crossed in love, and took it hard. He had never said a word about the incident or the girl—all I knew about it was what I'd heard from old Harry Phillips. Since then he'd behaved in a perfectly normal, friendly way with Pat Darrell, Leslie, Betty, and every other girl with whom he'd come in contact. But he seemed to have formed no attachments whatever.

He was pleased with the way things were going, like most of us. "Just two more months without anything serious going wrong," he said jubilantly, "and our troubles will be over."

"Why this high optimism?" I asked. "Can't you think of anything that might go wrong, Sammy?"

"I can think of a dozen things, but I don't think any of them are likely."

So as I left Sammy, thinking Leslie and Aileen had had long enough for their heart-to-heart chat, I was reflecting that things must be even better than I had thought if Sammy was so confident.

However, Leslie was alone and frowning thoughtfully when I reached our flat. "What's the matter?" I asked.

"Aileen isn't happy," she told me bluntly.

"Why not?"

"She's beginning to hate her father. And she's afraid of Morgan."

"Aileen? I think she's making a mistake, both times."

"How do you figure that?"

"Morgan isn't really big enough to be afraid of. He's a nuisance rather than a real danger."

Leslie shook her head rather impatiently. "We've been through this already. He's only a nuisance to you. But to Betty or Aileen, or anyone else weaker than himself, he can certainly be a danger. How about Ritchie? Why is it a mistake to hate him?"

"Nobody likes him, but he doesn't actually interfere with

194

anyone. He hasn't interfered with Aileen, or me, or you, or Sammy, or anyone else we know. If he did it would be different. Why hate a man who leaves you alone, who——"

"You're talking nonsense, Bill," said Leslie warmly. "I suppose you'd say if a man threatened you with a gun, that was nothing, that didn't matter, until he shot you?"

I grinned. "That's hardly an exact parallel, is it, honey?"

"Maybe I'm not logical," retorted Leslie, "but I'd rather be right than logical, any day. And I think I'm right about Ritchie, and that Aileen has good reason . . . But one thing at a time. Let's go back to Morgan. You say Aileen hasn't any reason to be afraid of him. Suppose you were Aileen. Would you like to be Morgan's girl?"

"She doesn't have to be."

Leslie appealed to the heavens. "Look, Bill. Didn't you people realize what you were doing when you abolished marriage?"

"What?"

"You were abolishing all sex crimes. There couldn't be any crime connected with sex any more—rape, adultery, bigamy——"

"Hey, wait a minute. Assault's still a crime."

"Is it? Suppose Morgan just carries Aileen off, like a caveman. Who's to stop him?"

I started to say something, but Leslie was in full cry. She very rarely got worked up over anything. When she did, however, she could swamp most people. She had quite enough intelligence to make all the right points, when she cared to use it. I could just see her as Portia in the trial scene.

"Betty doesn't matter," Leslie went on warmly, "since by abolishing marriage you've abolished bigamy. Aileen would say it was assault, Morgan and Ritchie would deny it. And who would Aileen appeal to? Ritchie's her PL. The council wouldn't pay any attention. They haven't any sympathy for people who want to stay single.

"So any time Ritchie decides to back Morgan, Aileen becomes Morgan's girl whether she likes it or not. Use your imagination, Bill. Don't just say it can't happen. It can. It will. Aileen's already asked to be transferred to some other group, and been turned down. What now?"

"I told you," I said patiently, "that Aileen didn't have to be Morgan's girl if she didn't want to, and I meant it. She can take Sammy instead."

"Say that again."

I did. Curiously, Leslie didn't seem to have thought of that. She hesitated for a moment, put off her stroke. Then she murmured: "That's the first sensible thing you've said."

Leslie had done us an injustice when she hinted that the lieutenants didn't know what they were doing when they abolished marriage. We were a people struggling to live, a people which must grow stronger and bigger. We couldn't afford to be concerned about the moral niceties of civilization. We weren't going to argue over bigamy, adultery, divorce, remarriage, desertion, and all the rest of it.

The only thing that did still deserve some attention, we thought, was the case where a man wanted a girl and the girl didn't want him, or vice versa. Sex freedom was all very well, but it had to be freedom for both. *Laissez-faire* isn't freedom—it's freedom for the strong, the determined, the persistent, and slavery for everyone else.

But someone pointed out that if A wanted B and B didn't want A, the answer was for B to find someone else.

So the PLs were told to deal sternly with assault, but with that principle in mind. In general, it was working very well. If someone, say, assaulted Caroline Stowe (not that that was at all likely, but the law must occasionally deal with hypothetical cases), and Caroline and John Stowe demanded justice, the man concerned would be very, very sorry he'd done it before the PLs concerned were finished with him. However, if some proud, beautiful girl, used to having her own way and determined to keep her figure the way it was, complained indignantly of assault, she was liable to be asked if she had some other man in mind, and if she hadn't, the offender was punished so mildly that he generally wasn't sorry at all.

I told Leslie some of this and she agreed that the lieutenants hadn't been such fools after all.

"We can hardly allow people to wait around for years to fall in love," I said. "I don't expect Sammy and Aileen are in love, or anything like it. This is a different kind of community from the one we left, and they both have sense enough to realize it. If they don't dislike each other——"

"I'm away ahead of you," said Leslie calmly. "We'll send them out tomorrow night before it gets too cold, to hold hands and generally get acquainted. You talk to Sammy first and I'll talk to Aileen. And maybe we can get the Morrisons in the next room to move out to one of the new flats lower down, more sheltered."

So after all this time of solitary grieving, drinking, hoping, fearing, and working, Sammy found he had a girl. It was a queer, bittersweet situation, the sort of thing that would naturally happen to Sammy. For there was no pretense about it—Aileen merely wanted a protector. She still thought she might be forced in the end to take Morgan, and she wanted to devalue herself, like a man gambling away a property because he hated the people who were going to inherit it. She would live with Sammy, but she told him—in our room, before they went out—with somewhat unnecessary frankness, I thought:

"I don't pretend I'm going to love you, Sammy."

"That's all right," said Sammy with similar frankness, "I don't think I'm going to love you either."

They laughed. "Well, anyway, you'll be better than Morgan," Aileen observed.

"If that's the best you can say for me," retorted Sammy, "I want a divorce."

They may have been more tender under the stars, when they went out to get acquainted. I didn't see how they could help it. When they had gone, I permitted myself for a moment to imagine myself in Sammy's place. . . .

"Enjoying it, darling?" asked Leslie tartly. I hear I'm not the first man to discover his wife is a telepath.

"I was just thinking," I said, "that on the whole I'd rather have you. Shall I tell you why?"

"Yes, please," said Leslie.

Later she said: "As a matter of fact they've been darned lucky, both of them. I don't know why either of them has been allowed to hang around single for so long, waiting for us to rub their noses together. As for the fact that they hardly know each other—you always claimed that you weren't in love with me, didn't you?"

"That," I said, "was when I was young and foolish."

Sammy and Aileen were as matter-of-fact about living together as they had been about discussing it. The Morrisons didn't move, but another couple near us did, and Sammy and Aileen moved in at once.

Aileen insisted on taking Sammy's name. "I don't like Hoggan much," she said, "but I like it a lot better than Ritchie."

That was the first time she made any public admission of how she felt about her father. We didn't follow it up, for she didn't invite discussion of the subject.

Thereafter she insisted on people calling her Aileen Hoggan and always called her father Ritchie, as if trying to pretend that there was no connection between them.

But she wasn't allowed to leave 92. Ritchie was the PL, and PLs had a lot of power—quite apart from the extra strings Ritchie could pull. Why Ritchie wanted to keep her in 92 wasn't clear. Apparently he said nothing whatever about Sammy—no comment, no congratulations, no protest. He simply ignored the whole affair.

I still thought, so help me, that Ritchie was overrated. People kept muttering about what a bad influence he was, how powerful he was becoming, how essential it was to find some way of checking him.

Undoubtedly he was a bad influence, but how much did he really matter? Not very much, I thought.

Which shows that even I didn't know everything.

7

It wasn't without reason that Leslie had said in those early days that there was always something worse on the way. Whenever you were over the hill—there was another one in front of you.

But we couldn't really rail against Fate, for every time we should have known about those hills. Every new thing we had to face was new only because we hadn't thought of it—not because we couldn't have known about it.

We should have known about the sun, back on Earth, long before we did, and we *could* have known; we knew some of it. We should have known that the lifeships we made could only be space buggies, and that it would be a labor of Hercules to get them safely to Mars. We should have known what would happen when a cold, dead world, its inner fires all but out, was suddenly and unevenly heated and thrown into climatic chaos. We should have known that people couldn't get on without some kind of exchange, and that our free, moneyless Utopia would soon be a glorious breeding ground for power-mad economic emperors. We should have known that if we had breezes and winds and gales we might any day have to withstand a great storm which was the grandmother and grandfather of them all.

And we should have known, before they happened, about the murders.

It was easy, the way we lived, to murder anyone in the settlement. That was demonstrated in one short, terrible week.

On Monday night Gregor Wolkoff, a member of 67, was found knifed outside the main entrance to bachelors' hall. There was uproar and horror, certainly, but nothing to what was to come. No real fear. It was a crime of passion, obviously, and soon the killer would be found.

In fact, quite a few people I talked to stressed the utter stupidity of the murder rather than anything else. How could anyone think for a moment he could get away with such a crime, cooped up in a small space with some eighteen thousand people, all of them watching for the faintest sign of the killer's guilt?

One of the reasons why Wolkoff's death was taken so lightly was that by all accounts it was no loss to the community. Some people, true, were horrified by the very fact of murder, which we had all thought we had left behind us. But most of the people who had known Wolkoff shrugged and said he was capable of anything and there might have been strong provocation. It might be a case of self-defense— though if that was so, we wondered, why was he stabbed in the back?

However, the situation changed completely after Wednesday night, when Jean Martine was found in the shadows among the parked ships, stabbed in the same way.

Jean Martine wasn't a member of a lifeship crew at all. He had been third navigator in one of the regular spaceships, and was of quite a different type from Wolkoff. He was young, popular, good-looking. Nobody knew anything against him. He had a girl, and no one knew of any other love affairs.

Aileen came flying into our room soon after we heard about this second murder, breathless, wild, and scared.

"Ritchie's behind this," she gasped. "What am I going to do?"

We couldn't get anything coherent out of her for quite a while. She was obviously hysterical, and I wondered whether I should slap her. But there are some girls you hesitate to slap, and Aileen, for me, was one of them. Leslie tried to soothe her, but without much success.

Sammy came in, saw Aileen, and said mildly: "Thought you'd be here. Aren't you supposed to be looking after Leslie? Seems she's looking after you."

Whether Sammy's handling of the situation was good psychology or not, it certainly had the desired effect. Aileen gulped and shook her head to clear it.

"You think I'm crazy," she said. "You don't know Ritchie. I do."

"How do you know he's concerned?" I asked.

"Because I know him," she said bitterly.

It's a funny thing, but when people are hysterical, particularly women, you discount what they say, even when, as in Aileen's case, you know perfectly well they aren't given to hysteria. We said soothing things, but if among them there was any admission that she was probably right, it was merely because that seemed expedient.

Two days later everyone was saying that Ritchie was behind all three murders.

That third one did it. The man who died this time was PL Venters, a known opponent of Ritchie, one he had never managed to pacify, involve, or cow. And suddenly it became obvious that the three murders were a part of some plan for power, and that the planner must be Ritchie. Now that it was obvious, people remembered that Ritchie and Wolkoff had been seen together a lot, and that Martine had spoken violently and tellingly against Ritchie. They also pointed out that though Ritchie had provided himself with an alibi for all three murders, Morgan Smith, his known ally, had no alibi at all.

Public opinion is often wrong, but I didn't think it was wrong this time. Now I believed Aileen. Now I knew I'd been mistaken about Ritchie.

So I was wrong. So Ritchie was a killer. So Aileen probably had good reason to hate him.

All I can take credit for is that when I knew I was wrong I admitted it fairly and squarely to myself and revised all my ideas about Ritchie and Aileen and Winant.

I didn't like what I came up with.

Some people wanted to string Ritchie and Morgan up without trial. If I'd been in charge of things, I'd have let them do it. We couldn't afford, yet, to be fair and impartial. It was, let's say, a sixty-five per cent probability that Morgan and Ritchie between them had killed all three people, and that was good enough. Even if we had the wrong people, this swift, decisive retribution would keep the actual murderers quiet for a long time. It wasn't the justice of civilization, it was the expediency of emergency.

Unfortunately, though, since we had such a big proportion of decent, fair-minded people among us, that was vetoed. Martian law wasn't going to start with hanging without trial.

"He knew that would happen," said Aileen listlessly. "Why don't people see that law doesn't prevent crime, it makes it easy for a clever man?"

The council passed a few more laws, and one of them made it clear that we weren't following the old principle of not trying a man twice for the same crime. We would try him, and keep on trying, until we proved his guilt or his innocence.

Then we tried Morgan and Ritchie for the three murders. We didn't even manage to make it look particularly likely that they were guilty.

But *they* did, by their attitude.

"You have nothing for us to answer," said Ritchie blandly, "nothing for us to deny, except that we murdered these three men. I can't speak for Morgan Smith; I can only say, for myself, I didn't kill any of these men, and you all know it. I don't see why I should bother to deny inciting Smith to commit a crime which no one has established he did commit."

"Why pick on me?" said Morgan resentfully, when he was called. "I'm only one of about five thousand people who *might* have stuck a knife in these three guys. Are you going to hang everybody who can't prove he didn't do it?"

And that was that. There was no evidence, let alone proof. We could only discharge them. We hadn't proved Morgan's innocence, but we certainly hadn't proved his guilt.

Nevertheless, a lot of people who had been uncertain before the brief, impromptu, abortive trial were quite sure after it. Ritchie and Morgan didn't act like innocent men. They acted, very deliberately, like guilty men who were quite certain their guilt couldn't be proved.

Unfortunately that wasn't evidence.

Very soon we found we'd played into Ritchie's hands. It was now generally known that he and Morgan were killers, and that nobody could do anything about it. Ritchie could use it as a threat. He did, almost openly. His power grew and grew. It was no use people saying he wouldn't dare. Obviously he would dare.

Before this I'd never had any actual demonstration of his power. Ritchie had never really seemed any concern of mine.

I had issued no contracts, nor had Leslie; there seemed no hold he could possibly have over us.

But when I made a serious attempt to have Aileen transferred to 94, I found out something of what Ritchie could do if he felt like it.

Leslie had her baby, a girl. We called her Patricia. The idea was Leslie's, not mine. I agreed without asking her whether she was thinking of Pat Darrell or not. At any rate, Aileen was so useful that Leslie felt we ought to do something for her, and what Aileen wanted was to get completely clear of Ritchie.

I thought her rather weak in this matter. You read of Trilbys completely dominated by Svengalis, but a normal person isn't so easy to dominate. All that was needed, I was certain, was that Aileen should take a firm stand and tell Ritchie firmly and without heroics what it was. However, there it was; Aileen thought she was in her father's power, and if she was to stop thinking so, someone else would have to take a hand.

I pulled all the strings I could think of to have Aileen declared independent of her PL, or transferred to another group, or anything else that would serve the purpose. Each time I was told, as I expected, "See So-and-so." On Mars people in authority were already back to the old game of refusing all responsibility, of passing the buck, of doing nothing rather than do anything wrong.

About every third time the person I was told to see was Ritchie, even if I hadn't mentioned Aileen by name. Apparently Ritchie had things arranged so that most changes had to be made, sooner or later, through him.

So I went and saw Ritchie. He had acquired one of the top flats, though he had no woman, and unlike the rest of us, he had all three rooms. That alone showed his power, wealth, and authority. He even had a stairway to the roof and had somehow managed to get part of it fenced off for his own private use. He probably saw himself as a millionaire with a penthouse.

Inside, too, there were many evidences of his special privileges. His flat was more nearly finished than any I had seen so far. He even had some rough furniture.

I ignored all that and went straight to the point.

"Why don't you leave Aileen alone, Ritchie?" I demanded.

"She's my daughter, Bill," Ritchie said gently.

"She doesn't want to be your daughter."

"She can't help it. It's an accident of Fate."

"What percentage is there for you in keeping her tied to you?"

Ritchie spoke in the same gentle tone: "I told you long ago, Bill, it wasn't money that mattered, but what you could get for it. I'm going to explain myself to you, Bill. But first I'm going to tell you why I'm doing it."

He sat back comfortably and looked at me. He was in no hurry.

"Drink?" he asked casually.

I shot a puzzled glance at him.

He reached behind him and from a recess in the wall produced a bottle and two glasses. He poured me out a drink and handed it to me. I sniffed it and sipped it.

It was raw, but it was alcohol.

"How the devil . . . ?" I began.

"Just drink it," said Ritchie. "I'll come to that. I'm going to show you a few more things, Bill. I'm glad you came to see me. I was going to ask you to come anyway, one of these days."

He downed the liquor and poured himself some more.

"What I want," he said, "is what quite a lot of people want. But I can get it. They can't. I want to be able to do what I like, eat what I like, drink what I like. I want to do things just to show I can do them. This, for example." He raised his glass. "I don't really give a damn for liquor. I can take it or leave it alone. But I like having it made, keeping it here. I like being the only man alive who can have a drink when he likes."

He smiled happily at me.

"I sell it too, of course," he said reflectively, "on a very limited scale. And it's no use thinking you can report that and have something done about it, because you can't."

He put the bottle away again.

"Now you wonder why I'm telling you this," he went on.

"I think I know," I said bitterly.

"Perhaps you do. You're thinking of fighting me, Bill. I strongly advise against it. I hate to mention Jean Martine as a threat, but in some ways Jean was very like you."

If I give the impression that Ritchie talked like an oily villain in very cheap melodrama, that's about right. The only thing he lacked was the unreasonable anger of such stage types. I don't think Ritchie knew how to be angry. He was always friendly, even when he was threatening your life. He had only one record to play. Friendliness, good humor, pleasure in your company—however false it all was, that was the invariable background music to anything his words might happen to mean.

"Soon I will have a very efficient bodyguard," Ritchie remarked. "Even now—Morgan!"

Morgan Smith appeared in the doorway. He had a gun in his hand, and he enjoyed pointing it at me.

"This is crazy," I snapped. "You get some scared chemist to supply you with alcohol, and there may be a lot of people who have made you silly promises, and you may control a lot of votes, but if Morgan shot me now a lot of people would dash in and you'd both be hanged. There's too much weight against you, Ritchie."

He nodded. "That's true. At the moment, anyway. No, if I really wanted to kill you, I'd have to arrange it another way. But it would be very little more difficult, Bill. You must know that. And I'm building up weight on my side. Morgan, send Edith here."

Morgan disappeared.

I got up. "I don't want any further demonstration," I said disgustedly. "No doubt this girl Edith will do anything you like. I'll believe that. I've also heard your threats."

Ritchie held up his hand in protest. "Edith works here as a servant, that's all," he said. "As far as women are concerned, I'm highly moral, Bill. I'm sorry marriage was abolished. I'm not in favor of these loose sex relations. Soon I'll have marriage reinstated, and then perhaps I might marry. But that's not what I want to talk about."

"I don't care what you want to talk about. I'm going. I take it you insist on making Aileen miserable to prove you can do that, too?"

"I'll always see," he retorted coolly, "that Aileen will have no real cause to be miserable. If she insists on pretending to herself that she is, I can't stop that. Just a minute, Bill. I expect you're even more determined to fight me now. Remember you have a daughter and a wife."

"You're threatening Pat and Leslie?"

"And you," he added easily. "If you yourself are a nuisance, it'll be you I have removed. But I know better than to try to scare you on your own account. Remember your daughter and wife when you think of doing anything."

I turned from him in white anger. A girl, Edith presumably, came in as I went out. I paid no attention to her, but I did notice she wasn't pretty. Probably Ritchie was as blameless from the sex point of view as he claimed.

Possibly also he was no sadist, unlike Morgan. Perhaps his deals were straight, according to the business ethics of dead Earth. Perhaps in many other ways he was blameless.

But none of that prevented him from being a fount of corruption, in a way I hadn't dreamed he was only a few days since.

Aileen was terribly right about Ritchie. She was right to be afraid of him.

Ritchie was still only a comparatively little man, despite his boasts. But there was nothing to stop him growing. He knew it. There would be a time when, if he and Morgan and I were placed as we had been, he could say casually, if he liked: "Shoot him dead, Morgan."

And Morgan could do it, then. Nothing would happen to

either of them. Ritchie, by that time, would have things organized his way.

Only now did I really understand how vitally important we lieutenants had been back on Earth, what an enormous responsibility we had had, and how two of us at least had misused it.

Lieutenant Porter had brought Ritchie along, and I had brought Morgan Smith. Porter was lucky—he wasn't going to see the consequences of his choice.

I was.

8

Betty didn't have a miscarriage, but her baby was born dead. We went to see her, expecting grief and hysteria.

We didn't see it. Betty was curiously calm and unconcerned. I think she had known all along that she would lose her baby, and that it would break her heart.

Leslie and I were silent as we left the hospital. Leslie wasn't back at work yet, but it would be only a day or two before she was. Eventually on Mars human beings would probably lose a lot of their physical strength through not taking enough vigorous exercise to develop it. Meantime, however, a person who would have been weak on Earth was quite capable of vigorous movement on Mars.

We were silent because we had seen a girl who had lost everything, and because we knew what it had done to her. Betty was too heartbroken, too lost to cry, to be anything but calm and apparently unconcerned.

It wasn't what had happened to Betty that mattered. If Leslie had lost me and then her baby, it wouldn't have finished Leslie. She would have cried violently, been miserable for a while, and then started to build new things into her life to replace what she had lost.

Betty wasn't going to do any rebuilding. She didn't have Leslie's capacity for that. What wouldn't have broken Leslie or Aileen or Caroline had broken Betty once and for all, beyond repair. We knew that, and didn't want to talk about it.

Presently Leslie deliberately dragged her mind and mine off Betty.

"Now we must see about giving Pat a little brother," she said brightly.

I protested. I had no quarrel with the idea in general, I said—not in the least. "But I want to have my beautiful wife just the way she is for a little while," I added.

I hadn't told her what Ritchie had said. I didn't see what good it would do to tell her.

A few days after Leslie came back to work, the food in the settlement began to improve. There could have been a general improvement before if all the extra supplies hadn't been passed on to pregnant women. Now there weren't nearly so many, and the diet of Winant in general slowly improved in both quantity and variety.

The exploration parties had paid off. They found no vast tracts of arable land, certainly, but they found a lot of little bits. Quite a few groups were taken away to work elsewhere —by spaceship, of course. That was the only means of transport we had.

The cattle were allowed to breed, a few of the older bulls were slaughtered, and there was a little fresh meat at last.

Eggs remained in short supply for a while as chickens were hatched. There still was scarcely any milk, but it would be only a matter of time before there was plenty for everybody.

The weather was becoming much more predictable. For one thing, the climate of Mars was still settling after the big change that had come over it. For another, we were becoming more used to the signs, and what had been, at first, storms completely without warning now gave us enough advance information to enable us to gauge their intensity.

We eased off a little in our work. It was too hot in midsummer, as it was now, to carry on with the same backbreaking labor. And the urgency wasn't as great now. We had turned the corner as far as the agricultural and accommodation problems were concerned.

Instead of devoting all our energies to providing rough-and-ready new accommodation, we now had half our force employed on refining what had been started. Slowly the cliffs were being faced with concrete, the various levels reinforced, lined, floored. We were no longer primitive cave dwellers. Our flats were beginning to resemble what we had been used to back on Earth. We couldn't paper our walls or finish them in wood, and we had no material for curtains or slip covers. But we had plenty of plaster and paint, and gradually the right plastics were being evolved to replace the cloth and leather we wouldn't have for a long time.

Landmark after landmark was passed. We had electric light long before we had water closets and taps and baths. However, these came at last. For a time we had electric radiators in the rooms. Then these disappeared and the whole block of flats had an efficient electric heating system. Big windows were put into the front rooms. None of them opened. We weren't going to make the mistake that had been made so often in Earth buildings, the mistake of having two independent and incompatible ventilation systems.

There were no outside staircases. At one time we had had to climb to our caves over the cliff face, and in high winds two or three people had been blown off the crude ladders and killed. Now there were ten broad stairways in the interior of the block, behind the flats. Soon there would be elevators.

Old maids' hostel was cleared away—there weren't many spinsters left. We now had five thousand flats at least started, some of them almost finished.

The future would have been bright if it hadn't been for Ritchie. He was still working assiduously at his self-appointed job of undermining everything that was done, with considerable success. I saw that clearly, now that I had stopped underestimating him.

The work parties were gradually dissolving. I hardly ever saw Morgan now. I knew he was with Ritchie most of the time. And Aileen didn't have to have much to do with 92 or with Ritchie. Occasionally PLs had to report on their parties, and they were still held responsible for their people. However, the emergency period being almost over, there was more freedom for everyone. Whether it was a good thing or not, our daily life was becoming more and more like what it had been on Earth.

In the council it was becoming harder and harder to get anyone to commit himself over Ritchie. I could understand that only too well. I was only one of many PLs who didn't want to oppose him too conspicuously. I didn't fawn on him. There was no pretense that I approved of him in any way.

But I didn't dare risk Leslie and Pat.

Though Ritchie was as strong as an ox, he had never done any work in Winant. First there had been his broken leg, and when that was no longer an excuse he had got round a doctor and had himself declared unfit for hard manual labor. Later still he had too much power for anyone to be able to do anything about him.

His top-floor flat was now a well-appointed suite, at least five times as luxurious as any other dwelling in Winant. With him or near him lived Morgan and a dozen other men whom he seemed to control absolutely.

212

The effect of the luxury in which Ritchie lived was much more serious than it appeared on the surface. Everyone knew that Ritchie had started off level with them. They saw the gulf that had opened between him and them, and resented him, hated him, feared him, admired him, envied him.

Only two others in the whole community had accomplished anything remotely resembling what Ritchie had accomplished. They were Giuseppe Bonelli and PL Smythe, both opportunists like Ritchie, though not in the same class.

However, it's not worth saying much about Bonelli and Smythe, for just about the time when they were coming into prominence, Ritchie had them murdered.

Just like that.

This time, of course, Ritchie himself had an absolutely unshakable alibi. He had been on his sunroof with twenty other people, hand-picked as reliable witnesses. Morgan didn't have as good a natural alibi, but he had a perfectly sound bought one.

Of course we were fools to let Ritchie get away with it. We should have strung him up without trial if we could. But who was going to be the ringleader in a scheme like that, which might fail? Who was going to be known as the man who tried to get Ritchie hanged?

Not I.

One evening I met Morgan in the passages, and to my astonishment he grinned at me. I didn't want to have anything to do with him, but I was so surprised I stopped.

"Okay, Bill," he said. "We fought long enough."

I waited.

"You brought me here," he went on, "and I'm grateful. I didn't like you when you could push me around. Now you can't. No one can. You can shake or not, as you like, and I don't give a damn."

He held out his hand.

"I'd shake, Morgan," I said, "if I thought we could both really mean it."

"What do you mean?" he asked quickly, with a flash of the old resentment.

"I don't think you can honestly shake hands in friendship with anybody any more, Morgan. And I'm sorry for it."

"I've got plenty of friends," he snapped.

I shrugged. "No doubt."

Quickly he recovered his good humor. The whole act was obviously based on Ritchie. Morgan wasn't with Ritchie because he was afraid of him, but because he admired him. Ritchie was all he wanted to be. And if Ritchie never took offense, Morgan wanted never to take offense either.

"All right," he said. "But there's no reason why we should snarl every time we see each other, is there?"

"None at all," I said civilly. "I'm not snarling."

And then on impulse I made what I knew was my last appeal to Morgan.

"Morgan," I said, "if you're carrying on the way you're doing because you think it's too late to do anything else— don't. You can always start again. Always."

"You mean——"

"I mean if you've killed men, that doesn't mean you must always be a killer. It's never too late. The people you're moving among now probably sneer when anyone says anything like that, but sneering at a thing doesn't make it false. It isn't too late for you, Morgan."

He hesitated, uncertain. He had lost his angry defiance. He seemed to be open to reason again, which he hadn't been the last time I talked to him.

"What could I do?" he asked almost defensively.

"I don't know. You'd have to find that out for yourself. But you could do something. And Betty would help you."

"Betty?" He stared at me for a moment as if he didn't know anybody called Betty. Then he laughed, not bitterly but with real mirth. "Betty!" he exclaimed, and laughed again.

He was still laughing when Betty herself came hurrying upstairs. I looked at her in surprise. Instead of plain work clothes she wore a soft blouse and a long, pleated skirt which swung gracefully about her thin legs. She was very attractive.

"I was looking for you, Morgan," she said.

214

"Okay," he said. "Let's go." He grinned at me, and they went off together.

I went to our flat, puzzled. The last I knew of Betty and Morgan, just after she came out of the hospital, they had been complete strangers. Yet they had gone away arm in arm.

It looked as if Ritchie had changed his mind, and as if Morgan, knowing he couldn't have Aileen, was making the best of Betty.

It looked that way for just six hours. Late that night Aileen came quietly into our flat with Sammy. Though they were quiet, I knew at once that something was very wrong.

"Ritchie has made up his mind," she told us. "I'm to marry Morgan—marry, you'll notice. I'm to do it willingly or else."

Leslie started to speak, but Aileen went on in the same controlled voice. "He didn't stop there. He told me or else what."

First, Sammy would die. Then Leslie. Then me.

Ritchie meant it. At first shrewd and careful, he was becoming drunk with power. He realized he had the power to do almost anything that crossed his mind—and what good was power if it wasn't used?

"He told me," I said. "He does things just to prove he can."

Aileen nodded. "He got the idea of marrying Betty," she said. "Yes, Betty. Your Betty. He wants to marry her and make her happy. So he's giving her everything she asks for, and——"

"Betty!" I exclaimed. "Then that's why she went with Morgan. What's her point of view on this—marrying Ritchie?"

Aileen shrugged. "She doesn't care. She doesn't care about anything. I think she goes to the flat just to be near Morgan. That's over, really—even for her it's over. But she still has to see him."

She dismissed Betty with a gesture. "You know," she went on, "it never crossed my mind until tonight that Ritchie was mad. Even now I don't think he is, except in that one thing. If you do mad things, even things you don't want to do, just

215

to show people you can do them, you're crazy, aren't you?"

"What happened, Aileen?" Leslie asked.

"It was a party. They got me there, and Sammy——"

"It was easy enough," Sammy said quietly, bitterly. "Morgan came and pointed a gun at us, and we went."

"Ritchie doesn't like wild parties," Aileen went on. "But then, you see, he was showing some friends and a few other PLs and some people he hasn't quite got in his pocket what he could do. It was the wildest party that anyone ever threw. Everything happened, short of murder. He keeps his murders discreet, and there was nothing discreet about this. You were nearly there, Leslie."

"Huh?"

"Oh, you'd have come, just as we went. Somebody suggested getting you to come and making you dance naked——"

"For Pete's sake!"

"And you'd have done that too. You'd have realized it didn't really matter beside the threats Ritchie would have used, and meant. But Betty vetoed it. That was the only crazy thing that was stopped, though, and it was only half stopped. I had to stand in for you."

"You don't mean," said Leslie incredulously, "that Ritchie made his own daughter——"

"You're missing the point," said Aileen coolly. "Ritchie is the boss. Nobody shares his power with him, though he may give in to Betty on a point or two. I don't matter any more than anyone else. Only he matters——"

"He *is* crazy," said Leslie. "I see the pattern, but it's a crazy pattern."

"Maybe. Anyway, we needn't talk about the other things that happened, sane or insane. None of that makes any difference any more, and Ritchie is going to stop being a nuisance or an emperor or a terror or whatever he is. If nobody else is going to do anything about him, I am."

I looked at Sammy, but there was nothing to be learned from him. He was looking broodingly at Aileen.

"Killing is nasty," said Aileen in the same quiet, controlled

216

tone, "and killing one's own father is so much nastier that I didn't even consider it until now. But it's got to be done. Already he has guards. Soon there'll be more of them. I'm one of the few people left who can get close to him. You couldn't, Bill. Sammy couldn't."

She took a deep breath.

"I'm going to kill him, but I don't want to die. I don't think I deserve to die for it. Will you help me? Will you lie, knowing people will believe you?"

Sammy had called me a tough nut, and perhaps he had had some reason. I said without hesitation:

"I'll help you, Aileen. I'll lie."

Leslie and Sammy and I were watching, on the ground. Ritchie, Morgan, and Aileen were on the sunroof—occasionally we saw one of them. With luck, we were going to see a murder.

The most plausible accident that could befall Ritchie was to fall from the sunroof to the ground. Everyone could believe in an accident like that—or make himself believe it.

We had argued, but Aileen and I were stubborn. Neither of us could see that it was wrong, or cared even if it was. If, back on the lifeship, I had known what Morgan would do later, I'd have seen to it that he never reached Mars. I'd have made sure something happened to him, something fatal—and I wouldn't have felt I was a criminal. There is, after all, a great difference between execution and murder. Aileen was executing Ritchie, knowing he deserved execution, knowing someone had to do it. She was probably right, too, when she said she was one of the few people who *could* do it.

Sammy wasn't so happy about it. "I wish I were God," he muttered, as we waited. "Then I'd know what was right. What an infernal situation . . ."

He stopped abruptly as we saw a head moving. It disappeared again.

The pit was now so deep that we could make out very little at the top. When people came close to the waist-high stone parapet we could see their heads and shoulders, and their legs through the spaces in the stonework. Unless they were close we couldn't see them at all.

In the circumstances there could be no warning. We couldn't see what led up to the incident we were to misreport. Our bias would be known, of course—but who would care? Who would speak up for Ritchie? Who would be sorry if he died? Who would try to prove we were lying?

Presumably Aileen would be working patiently to get rid of Morgan, whom we knew to be present on the roof.

"It's a mad scheme," murmured Sammy. "Ritchie knows everybody hates and fears him. He knows Aileen would be glad if he were dead. He won't be such a fool as to——"

"Look!" Leslie screamed.

It looked as if Sammy was right. We saw two men and a girl struggling on the edge. What had gone wrong we didn't know. But clearly Aileen had moved too soon, made a mistake, given herself away—or Ritchie had been expecting her attempt, waiting for it.

Anyway, she was going to fail. Her only chance had been surprise, to get Ritchie to the edge unsuspecting.

"I'm going up there," said Sammy desperately.

"Wait!" I said.

It was two men against a girl. Perhaps the two men, knowing that, were careless. Perhaps they forgot that though their strength was still overpoweringly greater than hers, the thrust of her legs was enough to raise all three of them quite easily against the 0.38 gravity of Mars.

Struggling in Morgan's grip, she lashed out with one foot. Through the gaps in the stonework we saw her leg whip up straight, so fast that it was a blur, and though a support blocked our view we winced involuntarily as her toe sank into Ritchie's belly.

On Earth that kick would have winded Ritchie, perhaps injuring him seriously. But this wasn't Earth. It lifted him perhaps two feet. He crashed back against the parapet, prob-

218

ably breaking his back. That didn't stop him either. His legs came up and he somersaulted over, turning in the air.

Instead of watching the roof, as we should have done—for Ritchie was already as good as dead, and didn't matter any more—we watched him, unable to look away, even when he struck the ground sickeningly.

When we looked up again, Morgan had both hands on Aileen's throat, and from the way his shoulders were hunched we knew they must be biting deep. Morgan was loyal to Ritchie to the end, apparently. He wanted revenge for Ritchie more than he wanted Aileen.

Then with a lithe backward flip Aileen wrenched Morgan off his feet and her shoulders back over the parapet. She must have put all her strength into it. Morgan sailed over, screaming.

She went over too, of course.

Sammy moaned even before they struck the ground. I knew what he was thinking. He had lost two women he loved, one on Earth and one on Mars.

Despite the horror of the thing, despite Sammy's pain, I couldn't help feeling a sense of relief. Even if it had to be grim and bloody and melodramatic like that, Mars was the better for it.

There was a thin cry from above. We looked up. Leslie gasped and shaded her eyes, screwing them up to see better.

"I think that's Aileen!" she exclaimed.

"Then who . . . ?" I began.

"It *is* Aileen," Sammy shouted.

We waved to her, and ran to where Morgan had fallen. We winced as we looked at them. His hands were still around Betty's throat.

9

We could only guess at Betty's state of mind. From the timing, she had obviously guessed what Aileen intended. Whether Betty had meant all along to kill Morgan or had done what she did in a sudden frenzy was anybody's guess. At any rate, she had sent Aileen inside for something, and when Aileen came back there was no one on the roof.

Very likely, as Sammy had said, Ritchie distrusted Aileen. But neither he nor Morgan seemed to have any distrust of Betty. We found it ironic, when we tried later to reconstruct the incident on the basis of all we knew, that Ritchie had probably been trying to save Betty from Morgan when she kicked him. Betty must have made some move against Morgan. That would probably only amuse Ritchie. He would have gone forward to break Morgan's grip. And Betty kicked him over the edge.

But these were only guesses. Aileen had meant to kill, and hadn't had to.

"I can't say I'm glad things have happened this way," she said. "I——"

"You can't say it, but you are," Sammy observed.

"I know *I* am," Leslie said. "Betty's life wasn't any good to her."

We still had big problems, we still had a struggle to live on a world that wasn't our own. However, it was nice to get on with it without the knowledge that we were always in danger of being stabbed in the back.

Sammy was in a daze for nearly a week. The certainty that it had been Aileen who had died had really shaken him. It was no use pretending after that that he didn't love her.

"Why are some people ashamed of perfectly decent emotions?" Leslie marveled. "Do you think Aileen will laugh at you for loving her, Sammy? If so, you haven't learned the first thing about women—the very first thing."

"Hell, Leslie," Sammy protested, "don't you start."

"The truth is," Leslie told him, "you don't believe in happy endings. It doesn't seem possible that Aileen is safe and prepared to love you and be loved, does it?"

"Let us have no more talk of love," Sammy ordained. "Love is a feminine myth, invented for the benefit of females. It's always women who talk of love."

With Ritchie removed, the Martian settlement moved on more surely, more in step, more cleanly. No one took on Ritchie's mantle. Now that he was dead, people spoke freely about him and his works.

There was a startling change. Startling, that is, if you don't know human beings. Apparently Ritchie had had no friends.

Apparently no one had ever liked him or supported him in any way. Apparently no one had ever been afraid of him.

The whole of Winant, it seemed, had been just about to put Ritchie in his place. There were suddenly all sorts of things that could have been done about Ritchie. Obviously, by being killed, he had merely escaped what was catching up with him, and would have caught up with him if he'd lived a few days longer. . . .

Lieutenant Porter and I had both made mistakes. Fortunately they canceled each other out in the end.

My group was what it should have been all along, a sound and healthy body of people. With Aileen in it, and Morgan out of it, it was a group of people who liked each other, could get on well together, and believed in the same sort of things.

"Of course," said Sammy, "this is only the beginning. Look at what we've had to face in the last year or so. Take the supremely optimistic view and say that this year things will only be half as bad——"

Leslie yelped involuntarily. "Aileen, shut him up, for heaven's sake," she exclaimed. "Sammy being supremely optimistic—like that—is just about enough to make me want to go away in a dark corner and cut my throat."

"I *am* being supremely optimistic," Sammy insisted. "Oh well, if you all want to live in a fool's paradise, don't let me stop you."

"I won't, anyway," said Aileen quietly. "There never is an ending, Sammy, we all know that. But there are turning points, and afterward when we look back we see how we were going down and down and down, until something happened and we started coming up and up and up. I think that's where we are now."

"Well, sure," said Sammy. "Didn't I say that things this year will only be half as bad as they've been so far?"

Sammy was right, and we all knew it. But we refused to listen to him all the same.

"You belong in the Old Testament," Leslie told him.

I grinned. "And Sammy begat Ahab," I said. "And Sammy begat Rebecca. And Sammy begat——"

Sammy and Aileen fled.

"And Bill begat . . . ?" Leslie suggested.

I think you could justifiably describe the way we kissed as supremely optimistic.